# *Taryn Leigh Taylor*

---

## *Kiss and Makeup*

NATASHA –

HAPPY READING !

◆ **HARLEQUIN**® BLAZE™

Recycling programs
for this product may
not exist in your area.

ISBN-13: 978-0-373-79870-4

Kiss and Makeup

Copyright © 2015 by Taryn Leigh Taylor

**Printed in U.S.A.**

**Taryn Leigh Taylor** likes dinosaurs, bridges and space, both personal and of the final-frontier variety. She shamelessly indulges in clichés, most notably her Starbucks addiction (grande-six-pump-whole-milk-no-water chai tea latte, aka: the usual), her shoe hoard (I can stop anytime I...ooh! These are pretty!), and her penchant for falling in lust with fictional men with great abs (Roarke, Harvey Specter, Kid Chaos, Dean Winchester and so on, ad infinitum.) She also really loves books, which is what sent her down the crazy path of writing one in the first place.

Want to be virtual friends? Check out tarynleightaylor.com, facebook.com/tarynltaylor1 and twitter.com/tarynltaylor.

To my family—

Mom, for keeping me sane (and for believing in me always, no matter what),

Dad, for inspiring me ("You should add a kid with glasses. And a dragon."),

and Logan, for keeping me honest ("Are you writing? Because that doesn't look like writing.").

And to my friends—

Crystal, you know I couldn't do this without you, right? We brainstorm together, we split...70–30, plus you get the benefit of reading the stories no charge (that's very fair);

Michele, this story is published because of you and I'm forever grateful;

and Michelle, thank you for teaching me to never ever give up on a dream. Ever.

# 1

"Do you want me to kick the crap out of that seat back and tray table for you?"

Chloe Masterson looked over at Window Guy, the man that the Goddess of Economy Airline Seating had seen fit to plaster against her right side. The upper-arm contact had started in Seattle and lasted until Chicago. Thanks to bad weather, their scheduled forty-five-minute layover in the Windy City was now pushing two hours, and had featured a long wait in the plane deicing line and then a "that didn't sound good" *thunk*. The plane was now sitting motionless on a vast expanse of snowy tarmac and they'd officially hit the six-hour mark of their touching-a-stranger marathon fifteen minutes ago.

It wasn't his fault, really. Window Guy had broad shoulders, so the contact was incidental and, in a weird way, kind of comforting. She liked that the sleeve of his gray wool suit was soft and warm against her skin.

And okay, *maybe* she was leaning against him a little more than was *strictly* necessary. Not because he smelled of spicy soap and warm man—which was a pretty wicked combination—but because he smelled better than the guy to her left. The gag-inducing aroma of stale sweat, onions and something else she couldn't quite place but preferred to leave a mystery had worn her down about twenty minutes after boarding. That's when Chloe had decided that the comfort of her left elbow wasn't worth permanent olfactory damage and had conceded the battle of the joint armrest to him.

*Damn middle seat.*

"Sorry?"

Despite their close confines, she and Window Guy hadn't exchanged more than the official "that's-my-seat" gesture of air travelers the world over before he'd awkwardly shuffled past her to sit down. After that, he'd pulled his laptop out and tapped away at the keys like a good little company automaton while she'd worked her way through a few chapters of a gently-used Stephen King novel. She'd been so engrossed in her book, she hadn't noticed that at some point he'd put the laptop away and moved on to reading the offerings from the seat pocket in front of him.

And that wasn't all she hadn't noticed.

Now that she was actually looking at him, his breach of their companionable silence was even more surprising. Because Window Guy was kind of sexy. Bedroom eyes the color of whiskey and twice as potent. A strong jaw and a straight nose. His brown hair was short enough to be business-appropriate, but long enough to get mussed up under the right circumstances. And that mouth! As she took her fill of him, it pulled slightly up at the right corner in an easy smirk that was hot as hell. He was the clean-cut kind of handsome that came with no visible neck tattoos and an expertly-knotted blue silk tie that bespoke gainful employment.

Men like him didn't talk to women like her. He was way too...corporate. And she was...not.

At her question, he raised his chin at the worn gray vinyl seat back in front of her. "You've been giving that chair dirty looks for the last twenty minutes, and then you sighed," he explained.

"I did?"

Window Guy nodded. "The sigh was pretty loud, actually. It disturbed my reading."

"Oh. Well. I'm sorry that my sigh threw off your concentration." Chloe sent a meaningful glance toward the airline safety pamphlet on his lap.

"The damage is done." He picked up the tri-fold piece of card stock. "It was just getting good, too. After the cabin depressurized, the plane crashed and the passengers were proceeding in an orderly fashion for their lives!"

*Huh.* She hadn't expected funny. Hot guys rarely had to develop such plebeian talents. "Sounds intense."

"You're telling me. I was really enjoying it until the author got all kinky and made the heroine take off her high heels before she used the inflatable slide. I think he might be a foot fetishist." He shoved the pamphlet back in the seat pocket in front of him before he met her gaze with a teasing glint in his amber eyes. "Wow. Spoiler alert. I hope I didn't give too much away."

"No, I appreciate the recommendation. I'll be sure to tell my book club about it."

His grin was practiced, but appealing. "I'm Ben."

Uh-oh. Time to nip this in the bud. "Well, Ben. You're a very handsome guy, and I appreciate the effort, because I'm sure that maneuvering a sober pickup with only a safety card, an in-flight magazine, and an airsickness bag as props is a challenge that few men could meet. But don't waste all your sweet, panty-dropping material on me. Save some of that A-game for Stewardess Barbie over there."

They both looked at the perky blonde flight attendant who'd been making doe eyes at Ben since he'd boarded. Right on cue, she twirled her ponytail and glanced away coyly.

Ben shifted, trying to arrange his large frame more comfortably in the tiny chair—a futile cause. "Let's get one thing straight here, if this had been a pickup, we'd already be—" he eyed his Rolex—*so cliché* "—three minutes into you becoming an airplane-bathroom sex convert. Let the record show that we are both still safely buckled into our designated seats, *ipso facto*, I clearly wasn't flirting with you."

Ignoring the frisson down her spine—legal jargon always had that effect on her—Chloe raised a skeptical eyebrow.

"Okay, I was *kinda* flirting. But, it was completely recreational. Minor league stuff."

"Oh, please! Foot fetish references? That is gateway flirting. If I hadn't called you out, you'd have escalated to the hard stuff—asking me my astrological sign and telling me how beautiful my eyes are."

He laughed, and Chloe ignored the flare of pride at having elicited the sexy, rumbling sound. Not that she was flirting, either, mind you.

"Well, it's hardly my fault that your eyes really *are* beautiful. Emerald green, with golden flecks that sparkle when you roll them like that because you think I'm being cheesy."

"Oh. Well that's probably because you *are* being cheesy. At least the safety pamphlet pickup was original."

"Original enough to get your name?"

"Chloe," she relented.

"Nice to meet you, Chloe." He offered his hand again, and this time she accepted it.

His palm was wide and his fingers were long. He didn't molest her hand; it was just an acceptable, firm shake between new acquaintances. Even so, a phantom warmth lingered after he'd relinquished his grip, the kind that buzzed up her arm and sort of made her wish he *had* molested her hand, at least a little. Chloe rubbed her tingling palm against the thigh of her jeans.

His gaze held steady on hers and his focus was flattering, almost seductive. If you went for that whole slick-successful-businessman-in-a-five-thousand-dollar-suit look. Which, she reminded herself, she didn't. Not anymore.

For the most part, her tiny diamond nose stud and purple highlights were enough to warn corporate wunderkinds that they had nothing in common with her.

But then she remembered that she no longer *had* purple highlights. She'd dyed her piecey, deconstructed bob for her sister's wedding. Right now it was a respectable, boring, *normal* shade of mahogany that skimmed her jaw before angling a bit lower in the front. The dye job was her attempt at a peace offering to her family. She just hoped it would be enough.

"…so if you look at it that way, cheese could be considered a high form of flattery, you know?"

Ben's voice snapped her out of a flashback of the most recent guilt-laden, middle-name-invoking phone call with her mother.

"What? Sorry. I wasn't listening."

Ben's grin was endearingly self-deprecating. "Tough crowd."

"It's not you." Chloe shoved her offensively monotone hair behind her ears. "Going back to Buffalo has put me in a rotten mood."

"That doesn't seem fair. What's Buffalo ever done to you?"

The derisive laugh slipped out before Chloe could stop it. "Now there's a loaded question."

Ben cocked a questioning eyebrow.

"I'm going to see my family." She didn't add "for the first time in four years," because that was the scary part, the part that turned her stomach into a churning pit of nerves and dread. "My little sister's getting m-married," she said, forcing the word out. Man, was it hot in here? She reached up and twisted the overhead air vent open.

"Oh! Well, that should be…" Ben paused in a way that let Chloe know she hadn't managed to hide her true feelings on the matter. He corrected midcourse, "no fun at all. Rings are like tiny shackles. Screw love. That's what I say."

It was a sweet attempt at a save, but Chloe was too far down the well to grab the rope.

"Weddings…" *Suck. Wreck relationships. Ruin lives.* She flipped through her mental thesaurus before going with, "aren't really my thing." She tugged at the front of her black T-shirt, but couldn't quite shake the sudden sensation of a phantom Swarovski-crystal-encrusted, sweetheart-necklined noose tightening around her rib cage.

Oblivious to her cold sweat and racing heart, Ben continued to aim for small talk. "It's a good thing you decided to fly in to Buffalo a few days early. This storm is really wreaking havoc on our arrival time."

Chloe shook her head. "I'm not early. She's getting married tomorrow."

Instead of the nauseating cheer that announcement had been garnering since her sister had started flashing her showy, four-carat diamond engagement ring around social media, Ben had the decency to look puzzled. Chloe appreciated that.

"Your sister's getting married on a *Thursday* in January?"

"You are only surprised by that fact because you've never *met* her," she informed him. "Anyone who knows my sister would expect nothing less from her than to inconvenience her entire network of family and friends by making them take a day off of work. Can't let a petty thing like the schedules of four hundred people interfere with her narcissistic, lifelong fantasy of having a winter wonderland-themed wedding on her birthday."

Ben nodded. "So you and your sister are close, then?" he deadpanned.

Chloe's smile caught her by surprise, but at least she could breathe again. He'd talked her down without even being aware of it. "You're a funny guy, Ben."

"It's a gift." He shrugged with faux modesty and loosened his sapphire-colored silk necktie. The hint of dishevelment made Chloe's breath hitch, but this time it wasn't the result of a chest full of anxiety. This feeling was warmer, and a little bit tingly.

She hadn't dated a man in a suit since Patrick—hadn't even looked at one. She preferred bad boys, the disreputable kind that parents didn't approve of. So why was Mr. Future Businessman of America giving her a serious case of the wobblies?

She didn't get a chance to scrutinize her odd reaction further. They both glanced up as an electronic chime sounded from the speaker above Chloe's head.

"Good evening, passengers. This is your captain speaking. Due to a mechanical issue and the impending storm, our scheduled flight has been canceled."

A collective groan filled the plane.

"Your flight crew will be handing out discount cards valid for a stay at any Value Inn location, a proud partner of Jetopia. Your boarding pass will be valid for tomorrow's rescheduled flight to Buffalo, weather permitting. If you have further questions or are unable to make the 8:00 a.m. flight, please speak with a member of your flight crew. Again, we thank you for choosing Jetopia, and we apologize for the inconvenience."

"What does he mean, *tomorrow*?" There was a definite note of panic in her voice, but Chloe was proud she'd managed not to shriek.

"I'm going to go out on a limb and guess he means the day after today."

"Hey, Ben?"

"Yeah?"

"That thing I said about you being funny? I take it back."

He waved it off. "As long as handsome panty-dropper still stands."

She couldn't even appreciate the joke—reality was seeping in. "I can't be stuck in Chicago. I need to get to Buffalo. *Tonight*." The wedding rehearsal and dinner were this evening. Her family would be expecting her.

Ben directed her gaze to the small oval window behind his head, and Chloe caught an ominous glimpse of the snow flying outside. "Better start walking then."

Chloe took a deep breath of musty cabin air tinged with eau de Aisle Guy's pits. *Trapped*. She glanced over as Ben liberated his iPhone from the breast pocket of his suit, thumbs flying over the screen as he, like so many other passengers, shared the details of this latest development with whoever was on the other end of the text message.

Chloe couldn't bring herself to do the same. She hadn't

even arrived yet and she'd already failed to meet her family's expectations. Not an auspicious start to her big reunion tour.

With another sigh, she flopped back in her chair, glaring once again at the seat in front of her.

She was stuck in Chicago.

With boring hair.

And an angry clan of Mastersons ready to pounce on her for the latest example of how she was ruining the hallowed family name.

This day could not possibly get any worse.

"You're doing it again."

"Doing what?" she asked, her eyes never wavering from the cracked vinyl seat back.

"Sighing maniacally," Ben explained.

"You seem awfully intent on the emotional health of complete strangers." She slanted him a look that bordered on caustic. "You're not a shrink, are you? Because my talking to a shrink would make my mother ridiculously happy."

"And how does that make you feel?"

In a defensive maneuver, Chloe crossed her arms over her chest. "Okay, fine. You're a *little* funny."

Ben pumped his fist in silent victory.

"And for the record, I was thinking about how Neil Diamond has ruined my life."

He shot her a surprised glance. "Really? I was wondering what he was up to these days."

She tipped her head in Ben's direction without breaking contact with the headrest. "It's a very sad story about a crappy alarm clock, a pathological hatred of 'Sweet Caroline', and an unfortunate mix-up involving the buttons marked *off* and *snooze*."

Ben leaned back in his own chair. "Fucking Neil Diamond," he said, and it was so understated, so unexpectedly perfect, that she laughed.

"You're pretty calm about this."

"About taking Neil Diamond's name in vain? Don't let the suit fool you. I'm surprisingly controversial."

Chloe shook her head, refusing to admit she was charmed. "Can't you just be pissed off about the flight being canceled? Like a normal person?"

His shrug was philosophical. "We're not getting to Buffalo tonight. Not worth getting worked up about if it's out of your control."

"That's very Zen of you," she said, though it wasn't a compliment.

"Fortune cookies," Ben sermonized, "are not only delicious, but full of extremely practical wisdom."

At that moment, Stewardess Barbie appeared beside Aisle Guy and her massive breasts exerted a gravitational pull on the eyes of the entire row, Chloe's included.

How did anything that top-heavy stay upright?

The flight attendant glanced down at her clipboard and Chloe couldn't help but notice that her glittery pink eye shadow was creased and caking.

Chloe fought the urge to tell her about the new eye shadow primer that Titanium Beauty had just come out with. It was oil-free and did an incredible job of keeping shadow in its place all day. And that glitter was best saved for evening events because mattes and neutral shimmers worked best in daylight or fluorescent light. Also that with her skin tone, peachier shades would be much more flattering than pinks..

"Gordon Hinky?"

Aisle Guy's gaze was stuck in the general vicinity of their messenger's more...*pneumatic* assets. Rolling her eyes at the predictability of testosterone, Chloe held her breath as he raised his arm.

Barbie sped through the "sorry for the inconvenience" script in a bored monotone before flicking her gaze to more promising territory. "And that must make *you* Benjamin."

*Gak.*

At least Ben had enough class to meet her eyes when he confirmed the obvious. "It's just Ben."

"Well, *Just Ben*, here's your Value Inn voucher."

Ben reached past her to accept the glossy slip of paper and Chloe caught the clean, masculine scent of him.

"It's good for fifteen percent off. There's a map on the back detailing the closest locations to the airport. Someone will be at the gate to direct you to the taxi and shuttle stands, but if you need any help finding your way or, you know, with *anything*, just say the word. I'd be *more* than happy to help you."

The breathy offer was very Marilyn Monroe.

"Jetopia apologizes for the delay, but we hope you'll give us the chance to make it up to you. We'd *love* to have you fly with us again." After a long moment, she tore her gaze away from Ben and focused on Chloe.

"And you're…" She glanced back at the list and her face fell like she'd just seen someone kick a puppy. "Oh." Her eyes darted between Chloe and Ben for a moment. Finally she said in a normal tone, "I hope you enjoy your stay."

"I'll need my voucher," Chloe reminded her.

"I'm sorry, Mrs. Masterson, but there's only one voucher per couple."

"Oh, I'm not a couple. And it's Miz. There's no Mr. Masterson."

"Actually…" Ben interrupted.

She twisted in her seat to find her handsome seatmate looking amused.

"*I'm* Mr. Masterson."

"What?"

"My name is Ben Masterson."

She stared at him for a long moment before turning back to the flight attendant. "I think there's been a *huge* misunderstanding."

Ben chuckled. "More like a *Mrs.*-understanding."

"Are you kidding me?" Chloe exclaimed. "A pun? Now?"

"Just trying to keep my sense of humor intact," he returned, unperturbed. After a beat, he added, *"Dear."*

"We just met," she pleaded, not trying to hide the anxiety in her voice. Chloe figured that an early-twenties poster girl for enhancement surgery probably understood a little something about desperation. "There's no way we're staying in the same room."

"My goodness!" Chesty McLookatmyboobs' attention focused on Ben with the precision of a heat-seeking missile, and her smile was one of renewed hope.

*So much for girl power.*

"I'm terribly sorry for the mix-up. I saw Ben Masterson and Chloe Masterson seated together on the passenger manifest and assumed… Well, let me find out what I can do for you."

"Give me a voucher of my own and we'll call it even," Chloe suggested.

"I'm afraid I can't just hand them out. For tracking purposes, I'll have to assign one to you in our system. It'll just take a second. I'm really sorry for the mix-up," she said again, more in Ben's direction, and sounding anything but sorry.

Chloe watched the flight attendant sashay down the

aisle and disappear behind the first-class curtain before she swiveled to face her last-namesake.

"This is your fault, you know."

He smiled apologetically. "I *did* set my weather machine to blizzard before I left Seattle."

"You're the one who rejected business class and deigned to sit with the common folk. No one would have assumed we were married if you and your Gucci suit had just stayed where you belong in the land of complimentary champagne and leg room."

"Hey, statistically, the seats in the back of the plane are safer than the first seven rows. And how did you know this suit is Gucci?"

Chloe ignored him and his designer suit, unaware that she was nibbling at her right thumbnail.

Her mother would *not* be pleased when she found out Chloe wouldn't be arriving until the day of the wedding. It was customary for the bride's family to present a united front at the rehearsal dinner. Especially if a certain daughter's absence would be duly noted and gossiped about.

She took a deep breath. Ben's fortune cookies were right. Dwelling on the disaster wouldn't change anything. Accepting that fact didn't change her mood, though. "So your last name's Masterson, huh?"

He nodded.

Crossing her arms, Chloe thunked her head against the headrest and closed her eyes. "Fucking Neil Diamond," she said.

As IT TURNED OUT, issuing another voucher did not "just take a second". The conspiracy theorist in her was convinced Boobzilla had purposefully slowed the process to make sure Ben was miles away by the time Chloe entered the terminal. Not, Chloe was embarrassed to admit, that she hadn't looked for him at the baggage claim when she finally made it there twenty minutes later, voucher in hand.

After grabbing her suitcase, she'd braved the icy roads in a crowded shuttle and was currently occupying the coveted "next in line" position in one of seven queues in the lobby of the Value Inn. Being this close to a shower and a bed had gone a long way toward taming her impatience. At least until the family of six ahead of her was told there was no room at the inn.

Chloe did a quick mental tally. Judging by the number of weary travelers still clogging the reception area, there were going to be a lot more disappointed people heading out into the snow tonight in search of shelter.

Chloe's grip tightened on the strap of her purse.

*Please don't make me one of them.*

When the balding desk clerk smiled at her, she stepped up to the counter.

"Welcome to the Value Inn. How can I help you tonight?" His voice was shockingly pleasant for a man dealing with a bunch of crabby, stranded nomads.

"Hi. Do you have a room for me?" They *had* to have a room left. She wasn't picky. She'd even settle for access to a sink and a cot in the hallway.

"Let me check what I've got. What's your name?"

"Chloe Masterson."

The clickety-clack sound of his typing stretched her nerves taut, reminding her of a countdown clock on a bomb. "Here we go. And that's for one night, correct?"

"Yes." The word came out like a sigh, heavy on the *s*, and Chloe's shoulders dropped to their normal position. She hadn't realized how tense she'd been.

"Okay, we've got you in room 224. Do you want a swipe key?"

Chloe raised her eyebrows. "I'll probably need one to get in the room."

Her sarcasm was lost on him. Nonplussed, he ran a plastic key through the card reader and handed it over with a smile. "Your room is on the second floor. Turn right when you exit the elevator."

Chloe paused in the act of unzipping her purse. "You don't need my credit card? Or my voucher?" She pulled the crumpled slip of paper from her coat pocket and held it out to him. "Because I went through a lot to get this."

"That won't be necessary. Your bill will be issued when you check out in the morning."

*Unbelievable.* "Oh, okay." Cursing Boobzilla's name, she shoved it back in her pocket. "Great. Thanks, then."

"Enjoy your stay."

She'd no sooner stepped away from the counter when the inevitable happened.

"Excuse me, folks," the clerk announced to the crowd. "I'm afraid we are all out of rooms for tonight."

Finally, *something* had gone right for her today. She hurried away from the outraged mob and into the elevator. The door slid closed behind her, and she was in such a good mood that she didn't even mind that the Muzak version of "Song Sung Blue" was playing during the short trip.

The room was as easy to find as Mr. Sunshine had made it sound, and she shoved the card in the door, ready for a shower and a bed, in that order.

Instead, she opened the door to find a hot guy pulling a white T-shirt over the most spectacularly muscled back Chloe had had the privilege to see this side of a movie screen.

*Oh, yum.*

The forgotten door banged shut behind her.

He turned and she caught a glimpse of six-pack abs before the white cotton swallowed them up. Then she raised her eyes to his face.

Her suitcase slipped from her fingers and landed with a muted thud on the carpet. They stared at each other for an infinite moment—both the longest and shortest seconds of her life.

"You've got to be kidding me," she said.

A full-fledged grin spread across Ben's face. "Honey, you're home!"

"I SHOULD HAVE KNOWN! The second that clerk didn't want my credit card or the stupid voucher I should have known." She stomped into the room like she owned the place, abandoning her suitcase where it had fallen, and then her purse and coat beside it. "Why does today suck so much?" she asked before flopping onto his bed, her feet still flat on the floor as she stared up at the ceiling.

Ben was pretty sure she wasn't talking to him. Which was fine. He was content just to look at her. To be honest, he'd hung around the baggage claim area for ten minutes after he'd grabbed his luggage, just in case she showed.

Ben had to admit, the pinup-girl-with-an-edge thing Chloe had going on—like some twenty-first-century Bettie Page—was working for him in a big way. Goth-rockers were not usually his type. As a general rule, he dated women who were soft and positive, not really the adjectives that came to mind when he stared at the pissed-off pixie glowering up at him.

"Your airplane girlfriend kept me in voucher limbo for so long that my suitcase was the lone bag circling the conveyer belt by the time I got to baggage claim. Then I almost missed the shuttle, and now this? There's not even a comforter on this bed."

"Oh. I took it off. Have you seen what happens when they shine a black light on hotel quilts?"

"That is gross and disturbing. But it's still weird you got rid of it."

What was he going to do with her?

He'd only struck up a conversation with Chloe on the plane to pass some time. And then she'd hit him with those liquid-lined, green-and-gold eyes and a bad attitude and he'd been all in. Kinda made him wish he didn't have so much work to get done tonight.

But if his meeting in Buffalo went the right way, he was going to be the new account director at Carson and McLeod. And a promotion meant a raise, and a raise meant the cabin on the lake would be his.

Still, he couldn't just throw her out. She wasn't plastic pretty, like the cookie-cutter blonde flight attendant she'd just alluded to. Chloe was sharp and smart-mouthed and real. She gave as good as she got, and he liked that about her. He also liked that, sprawled across his bed sheets in something as innocuous as a black T-shirt and jeans, she somehow managed to look provocative as hell. His body hummed with testosterone-fueled appreciation.

*Jesus, Masterson. Get a grip!*

You'd think he hadn't been laid in years, when it had actually only been—a depressing calculation revealed that it had been almost a year since his rebound fling after he and Melanie had imploded. He'd been so focused on work that he hadn't noticed how long it had been. Which was pathetic on many levels.

"What the hell am I going to do?" Chloe fumed. "They don't have any other rooms."

"You can stay here." The words were out before his brain had registered the consequences, but he didn't regret them. It wasn't even the testosterone talking. By all accounts, Chloe had had a rough day. She deserved a win. For once, work could wait.

Those amazing green eyes widened in surprise as she bolted upright on the bed. "What?"

"I mean, you're already here. I'm sure all of the airport hotels are in the same boat, so there's no sense heading back out into the snow. Besides, we're married, right?"

Her death glare was adorable. And just a front. She was considering it. She had a horrible poker face.

Chloe managed to hold out for seventeen seconds before she exhaled contemptuously. "If you snore, I *will* smother you in your sleep. Just so you're warned."

Ben did his best to tamp down the wattage of his smile. It was cute that she still thought she was keeping up her tough-girl facade.

"Excellent choice, Masterson." He grabbed his wallet from inside his suitcase. "You settle in here, and I'll go see if I can get us a cot and some food." Ben headed for the door. "If I'm not back by midnight, check the ice machine for my corpse."

Chloe might be having a really bad day, but his was turning out pretty well.

# 2

BEN MAY HAVE neutralized the no-shelter problem for her, but he couldn't help her with the Dragon Queen—her mother. She was going to have to slay that beast herself.

Chloe cast a covert glance at her purse, which was sitting on the floor where she'd abandoned it, about four feet away. *Just do it*, she lectured herself. *Woman up and stop putting off the inevitable.*

She heaved herself off the bed to retrieve her purse, grabbing her coat off the floor, as well. After she'd wasted a couple more seconds arranging her coat on the back of the desk chair and applying some ChapStick, there were no more stalling tactics left in her arsenal. With a resigned breath, she pulled out her cell phone and dialed the number she'd been dreading calling since the moment she'd realized she'd be spending the night in Chicago.

"Hello." The frigidity of the word let Chloe know that caller ID had already announced her identity.

She exhaled. "Hey, Mom."

"'Hey, Mom'? You're calling me during the rehearsal dinner where everyone is staring at the gaping hole where the bride's sister is supposed to sit and all you have to say is 'Hey, Mom'?" Fiona Masterson's voice was eerily calm. Which meant her mother was furious. "Everyone is wondering where you are."

She had no doubt that was true. Her sister's big day might be the main event, but more than a few of the attendees were waiting with gossipy glee to see the sideshow—Chloe's return.

"My flight got canceled. There's a really bad storm here in Chicago. I'm really sorry." Chloe paced the short length of the hotel room.

"This is why we wanted to buy you the first class ticket that would have gotten you here days ago, if you'll recall. To avoid just such a situation. You know winter weather is completely unpredictable. Never mind the fact that you've missed your sister's stagette, her bridal shower, her lingerie party, the family brunch, the luncheon for out-of-town guests, the—"

"I told you I couldn't get that much time off work. I'm really sorry I missed…all those things, but it's not as if I'm a bridesmaid or anything." *Thank God.*

Some people might have felt slighted by the oversight, but Chloe had been all kinds of relieved. Standing up at the altar in front of all those people… Just the thought of it was enough to give her PTSD. "And I'll be there for the wedding. I promise. Even if I have to hitchhike, I'll be there."

Her mother sighed, and Chloe hoped she'd sounded much less melodramatic when Ben had called her out for the same thing on the plane earlier.

"So help me, Chloe Marie, if you do not arrive in time for your sister's wedding…"

"Mom, I gotta go. I'll be there tomorrow around ten."

Chloe disconnected the call and sat heavily on the side of the bed.

What was it about talking to her mother that made her

feel like she was sixteen years old again? She'd moved across the country to escape the phenomenon. Yet all it took was a phone call to bring back all the feelings of being *less than*.

The tears caught her by surprise. They were followed closely by sobs that made her shoulders lurch. The more she cursed and fought the show of weakness, the more torrentially it manifested itself. After a while, she just gave in.

The sound of the door opening couldn't have startled her more if it had been a gunshot.

*Shit.* She wiped desperately at her puffy, tear-swollen face, trying to erase the evidence of her breakdown. The man had the worst timing of anyone she'd ever met.

"Chloe? You should have seen the lineup for the restaurant. It's a madhouse down there, so I had to improvise. Also, I added my name to the cot waiting list. Which is hilarious because— Hey, what's wrong?"

"I'm fine," she lied, willing him to turn around and give her a minute so she could pull it together.

He came closer. Chloe kept her eyes down and her body still, but he wasn't deterred by her attempts to ignore him. She hiccupped as he set an ice bucket on the nightstand and then sat on the bed beside her.

"I'm sorry. I don't know what's wrong with me." She shot him a watery smile, with every intention of leaving it at that. But when she saw the genuine concern on his face, felt the warmth of the reassuring hand he'd placed on her back, she spilled her guts.

"It's just, today has sucked," she said with a sniffle. "I'm talking *monumental* amounts of suckage, and I'm tired, and moody, and people have really been getting on my nerves. All I want is to go home, but I'm stuck sharing a hotel room with a complete stranger who must think

I'm mentally unbalanced. And you've been really nice to me anyway. And now I'm crying again. I *hate* crying," she finished on a shaky sob.

Ben reached past her to the nightstand and snagged a tissue, handing it to her.

"You see? You barely know me, you have every reason to believe I'm deranged, and *still* you have the decency to hand me a Kleenex."

"It's really not that big a deal."

"Yes, it is, Ben. You're nice. And you're tall. You're very tall." She wiped her nose with the tissue. "How tall are you, anyway?"

"Six-three."

"That is very tall." Chloe shook her head, looking down at her hands. She picked resolutely at the flaking black nail polish on her right thumbnail. She must have been chewing on it—she did that when she was stressed.

She expected him to bail then, distance himself from his sobbing lunatic of a roommate with some teasing remark about how tall guys are known for their big wangs or something equally ridiculous. She'd laugh, and he'd laugh, and they'd get back to the superficial banter that befitted two strangers stuck in a hotel room together.

But he didn't.

He just sat beside her, respecting the silence. And her thoughts slipped out. "Honestly, Ben. How is it possible for one person to mess up her life so monumentally?"

"Hey, I'm sure it's not as bad as it seems right now." He rubbed her back, his big hand hot against her T-shirt. "You'll figure it out. You'll fix it."

Tears brimmed in her eyes with a vengeance. They burned like acid. "No. I won't. And do you know why?"

Ben shook his head.

"Me, neither! I mean, do you see this? Do you see my hair?" She grabbed a handful and held it in his direction.

"Yeah…"

"I did this for them!" she exclaimed, dropping the strands back into place. "I colored it boring old brown so they wouldn't be embarrassed by me, but it didn't work! I'm not even at the wedding yet, and I've already disappointed them. Nothing I try ever works, Ben. I don't know what to do." She'd never said that to anyone before and admitting the truth hurt so badly she thought her ribs might crack.

Chloe dropped her face into her hands. Ben's arms came around her, pulling her close, tucking her cheek to his chest. She gave in and greedily took what he was offering. Wrapping her arms around his waist, she leaned into him and let herself cry.

She wasn't sure if it was minutes or hours, but he held her until she had no more tears.

"You know what, Chloe?" His voice was soft and deep, breaking the silence she'd been measuring with the rise and fall of his chest beneath her cheek. "Maybe there's nothing *to* do. I mean, I realize I just met you, but you seem okay to me."

That tiny reassurance allowed Chloe to muster enough gumption to reach up and wipe the wet tracks from her face. She couldn't quite bring herself to lift her head off his shoulder, though.

"And they'll see it. One day, they'll see it. You just gotta give them some time."

Her lip trembled, and she bit it, fighting the sadness. "They've had twenty-six years, Ben."

She felt him exhale. "It's a really hard thing, you know, not taking the people we love for granted." She looked up at him then and he smiled, a sad-but-reassuring little half smile that made her believe there was a chance that the despair she felt in that moment might not be insurmountable.

Chloe pulled away with a final sniff. She was trying desperately to hold onto that moment of comfort even as the embarrassment of her epic cry-fest in front of a virtual stranger began seeping in at the edges.

She exhaled shakily. "Sorry I got mascara and snot on your fancy shirt."

"It's just a T-shirt," he averred as he pulled the black-smeared wet patch away from his chest. He even managed not to look horrified.

"Yeah, but I bet it cost, like, fifty bucks."

"Seventy-five," he corrected. "But I'll accept it as punishment for being douchebaggy enough to have spent that much money on a plain white T-shirt in the first place."

Chloe's chuckle was waterlogged.

"C'mere," he said, tucking his thumb in the hem of his shirt. She leaned ever so slightly forward and let him rub the cotton-covered pad of his thumb under her right eye, then her left. She'd be surprised if she had any makeup on at all at this point. Some warrior, she thought, choking in battle and crying off her armor.

"There," he said, showing her the black smudges on the fabric. "All cleaned up."

She frowned, letting him know she wasn't buying his bullshit.

"Okay, you should probably go wash your face before we have dinner," he admitted. "Unless the raccoon look is a thing now."

Grateful for the reprieve, Chloe headed for the bathroom, pulling her suitcase into the tiny room with her. She groaned when she caught sight of herself in the mirror.

Apparently in addition to being an all-around good

guy and world-class hugger, Ben Masterson was also the King of Understatement. She looked like a comic-book villain whose face was melting off. Chloe shut the door and set her suitcase on the toilet, rifling through it for her toiletries case.

A couple of swipes of a makeup remover pad later, her cheeks were clear of black streaks, and her eyes were bare, if a little puffier than they had been this morning. She'd have liked to take all her makeup off and start again, but snotting all over Ben had been all the weakness she could handle. No way was she going to be barefaced in front of him. She didn't even start the makeup videos on her YouTube channel that way.

"Hurry up in there, Chloe. I'm starving!"

"Almost done! Don't eat everything!" She ran a brush through her hair, topped up her deodorant, and rooted around in her suitcase in search of her pajamas.

WELL, TONIGHT HAD certainly not been the typical room-service-and-work type of night that tended to dominate his business trips.

Chuckling to himself, Ben pulled off his T-shirt, wiping his shoulder with it before folding it up and placing it in the dirty laundry bag he kept in his suitcase. He'd say one thing about Chloe Masterson, she was the antithesis of boring.

A woman who couldn't decide whether to smile at him or punch him in the face. A woman who was super tough one moment, and vulnerable the next. A woman who had no idea her expressive face betrayed her, even in her most badass moments.

He tugged the white button-down he'd worn on the plane back on—she'd walked in on him before he'd gotten around to changing out of his suit pants, so it wasn't like he'd be overdressed—but he left the hem untucked and the buttons at his throat open anyway.

She was such a nice change from the women who'd inundated his world lately. As he'd moved up the corporate ladder, everything had gotten more proper and refined. So serious. He'd met a lot of very pretty women with very pretty plans for their future. The few dates he'd been on in the past year had felt more like job interviews, and they'd fizzled accordingly.

But Chloe didn't look at him as if he was a steak on display at a butcher shop. She wasn't angling for marriage, sizing up his earning potential or evaluating his parenting qualities. Which was good, because marriage was not high on his list of priorities anymore. She was the kind of woman who understood that a date should be fun and flirty, two people trying each other on. No expectations, just opportunity.

Not that this was a date.

In fact, he wasn't sure what this was, but he kind of liked it. Tonight he got to hang out with a flawed, stressed-out, hot-then-cold-then-hot-again woman with a kick-ass body, a pierced nose and a star tattoo on her right arm. And he couldn't wait.

He moved her abandoned phone to the nightstand so he could prop the pillow upright against the headboard, and sat down against it. He'd just stretched his long legs out in front of him when he heard the bathroom door open.

She appeared from around the corner a moment later.

Ben let his gaze slip from her berry lips down to her bare shoulders, then to her arms—that star tattoo was going to be the death of him, he was sure of it—lingering a moment on the way she filled out her tank top before sliding past her black boxer shorts to take in her truly spectacular thighs, her shapely calves and the shiny black polish on her toenai—

"Oh, my God, are you walking on hotel carpeting in bare feet?" he asked, lunging forward. "Do you have any idea how gross hotel carpet is?"

He was half expecting another sardonic smile, but apparently the panic in his voice had registered, because her eyes widened in response to his alarm.

"How gross?" she asked, scrunching up her nose in preparation.

"My grandma was a nurse, and she once had this patient who ended up with cellulitis from walking barefoot on hotel carpeting—"

"Are you kidding me?"

"—and he didn't get it checked right away, so by the time he went to the emergency room his whole leg was full of pus—"

"Ew, ew, ew!" She was hopping from foot to foot by this point.

"—and he had to stay in the hospital for three days so they could give him antibiotics intravenously."

"Okay, enough, enough!" She jumped onto the bed beside him, scrambling into a sitting position and staring down at her feet. "Oh, God! My feet are itchy. Is *itchy* a symptom of cellulitis?"

"Yes."

Her eyes went wide.

"Well, probably." He didn't remember *all* the details of the story...just the gross ones. "Do they feel swollen? Like there's a bunch of pus accumulating under your skin, getting ready to erupt and—"

Chloe recovered enough to sock him in the arm. "Shut up with the gory details, wouldja?"

Ben rubbed his arm where her punch had landed.

Chloe crawled over to the end of the bed. She braced one hand on the very edge of the mattress and reached toward her coat, which was hanging on the back of a chair that was just out of reach. Her fingertips brushed the thick material, but she didn't quite get purchase on it. He watched in fascination as she set herself up for another attempt.

"*What* are you doing?"

"I left my suitcase in the bathroom, and if you think I'm setting one bare toe on that hideous, infested carpet then you're way dumber than you look," she said over her shoulder.

He shot her a tight smile. *Ha, ha.*

"So I'm going to stand on my jacket, slide my way over to the bathroom, and get myself some socks."

"Or you could just ask me to get your suitcase," he pointed out, getting to his feet.

She gazed up at him with such wonder that he honestly believed the idea had never occurred to her. "I… You don't have to. I mean, I can do it myself."

"I'm sure you could, eventually. But I'm happy to help, because if you slip and contract cellulitis, the amputation would ruin your sister's big day." Ben smiled angelically and dodged when she chucked a pillow at him.

Her ugly suitcase was sitting on the toilet. "You should really have a lock on this when you're flying," he advised, grabbing the scratched-up plastic case and heading back into the bedroom. He dropped it on the suitcase stand and set it down beside her. She threw open the lid to reveal bedlam inside.

"You know, most people fold stuff before they put it in the suitcase, just FYI." Ben resumed his position on the bed beside her.

"Thanks for the packing tips." Her voice sounded less

than sincere as she hunted through the chaos. She rescued a ratty sock from inside the suitcase and jammed a foot into it. "Wow. That looks sexy." She stuck her foot in the air so Ben, too, could admire the purple, elastic-challenged sock that was slouched around her ankle.

"Yeah, well, it's sexier than athlete's foot."

"Amen, brother." She reached out to give him a high-five before quickly pulling on the other sock. She closed up her suitcase. "Okay, now that that's taken care of, on to more important things, like food."

He reached over to the nightstand and dumped the contents of the plastic ice bucket on the bed between them. An avalanche of candy spilled across the sheet. "Dinner is served."

"Whoa. What'd you do? Knock over a vending machine?"

"I wasn't sure what you'd be in the mood for—salty, sweet, *stale*," he offered, rapping a rock-hard, prepackaged Danish against the headboard with a disconcerting *tap, tap, tap,* "or all of the above—so I got one of everything." He lobbed the Danish at the trash bin on the floor beside the television stand. It landed inside the plastic container with a heavy *thud*.

She did that cute nose-scrunch thing again as she deliberated over the colorfully-wrapped mound of sucrose and diabetes. "SunChips, Skittles, Aero Peppermint. And I'm taking the cherry Life Savers," she decided, grabbing each of her picks from the junk-food dog pile as she named them. "You know, in case of emergency."

Ben nodded contemplatively, undoing the buttons at his wrists. "Those are some bold choices, Masterson." He rolled up his shirtsleeves in preparation for his own selection process. "Personally, I'm more of a traditionalist. I'm going for the Doritos with a side of Mike and

Ike, Jolly Ranchers to cleanse my palate, and Twix for dessert. You want to split the pretzels as an appetizer?" he asked, ripping into them and holding the miniature bag in her direction.

"Why not?" Instead of taking one pretzel, though, she took a handful, and Ben liked that about her. She balanced them in a precise stack on her knee. "So does the wife know you leave the ring off while you're away on business so you can lure pajama-clad strangers into sharing hotel-bed dinners?" she asked, crunching into a pretzel.

Ben shook his head. "Single and loving it."

Chloe's laugh was smug. "There's a shocker."

"So what about you?" he asked.

"What about me?"

"Well, I know you're a Masterson by birth because on the plane you said there was no Mr., but that still leaves plenty of options."

She shook her head as she started on the SunChips. "Also single. Mostly loving it, except when I'm on the phone with my mother, dodging the grandkid discussion. I did, though. Have a boyfriend. We broke up about five months ago. He cheated on me," she explained, answering his unspoken question. "A couple of times, actually. It was all very cliché. I have horrible taste in men. Spider and I were a mistake right from the beginning."

Ben choked on his pretzel. "You dated a guy named Spider?"

Chloe nodded.

"Wow. Was he a professional wrestler?"

"No."

"Did he have superpowers?"

Chloe rolled her eyes. "He owned a tattoo parlor."

"That was going to be my next guess." The chip she

hurled in his direction bounced off his chest and landed on the sheets. "So where did you meet *Spider*? Intermission at *La Bohème*? Church book club?"

"I met him when he gave me these." She set her chips on the pillow and reclined, tugging the waistband of her shorts down enough to reveal a pair of small birds etched just inside her hip bones, one on either side of her abdomen.

Ben almost swallowed his tongue. Christ, he ached to touch her. His hands flexed involuntarily, resulting in the decapitation of several pretzels unfortunate enough to be left in the bag he was holding. He set it on the mattress beside him and took a deep, steadying breath. And he'd thought the star on her arm was haunting him.

"Which is kind of ironic when you think about it," she continued, oblivious to his slack-jawed appreciation of her body, "because swallows mate for life." She snapped the elastic back into place and, instead of resuming her sitting position, she rolled onto her tummy.

*Is she commando under those shorts?*

"Anyway," said Chloe, reaching toward the pillow to retrieve her dinner as though her extreme hotness hadn't just evaporated every speck of moisture in his mouth, "I finally kicked his ass to the curb when I walked in on him and his latest conquest christening the kitchen table *I* paid for. And the rest, as they say, is history. How about you?"

Ben managed to work up enough spit to moisten his tongue. "I have never dated a guy named Spider."

"C'mon, Ben. I showed you mine." Chloe fished the last chip from the bag, crumpled the empty packaging in her fist and tossed it awkwardly over her shoulder in the direction of the garbage can. It hit the end of the bed and rolled onto the navy carpet. "Spill it. How did your last relationship go down in flames?"

Melanie's face flashed in front of his eyes. He felt like a dick for giving Chloe a hard time. He was the king of clichés.

The boss's daughter. The heirloom ring. The proposal eclipsed soon after by her announcement that she was leaving him. For some douchebag lawyer who was her father's age and had enough money to keep her in the style to which she was accustomed. They'd walked down the aisle six months after she'd ditched his ass. They'd recently celebrated a year's worth of wedded bliss.

Ben shook off the humiliating memory.

"Nothing to tell." Ben poured some M&M's into the palm of his hand and held them in Chloe's direction.

"Love 'em and leave 'em, huh?" she ventured, selecting the three red ones from the mix and eating them simultaneously.

Ben transferred the remaining candies from his palm to his mouth and gave her a "whatcha gonna do?" shrug. "What can I say, Chloe? I'm a lone wolf. I don't play by society's rules."

Smiling, Chloe tore open her Skittles. "Perfect. Then *you* can be the one to spike the punchbowl at the next family reunion. I'm tired of being the black sheep of the Masterson family."

He grinned. "Much as I'd like to be in on your diabolical plots, I probably won't be scoring an invite to the party. Grandpa and Grandma Masterson couldn't have children. My dad was adopted." He selected a blue M&M's from the package and tossed it in the air, catching it in his mouth.

She froze, sexy green eyes wide. "We're not twelfth cousins twice removed?"

The idea hadn't even occurred to him, but he realized now it had been dominating her thoughts. And why wouldn't it be? Unlike him, she couldn't have been sure they weren't related.

Something had shifted in the way she looked at him. It was a slight change, almost indiscernible, but he felt it in his gut. And a little south of his gut.

She took a deep breath and Ben was treated to an eyeful of cleavage. God, her breasts were amazing. His hands flexed again.

His pulse raced and Chloe's breathing grew shallower. Her lips parted.

The piercing cry of the hotel telephone jerked him out of the moment.

He fumbled with the bulky receiver before bringing it to his ear. "Hello? Yes, this is Ben. No, I only requested one cot. Yes, I realize the room has a queen-size bed."

His prey—or had she been the hunter?—took the opportunity to retreat, mouthing the word *shower* at him before grabbing her suitcase and disappearing.

SHE WAS IN BIG, big trouble.

Chloe tipped her head back and let the warm spray of the shower wash the remnants of the day and the smell of chemically-approximated flowers—courtesy of the Value Inn's complimentary two-in-one shampoo—from her hair.

This wedding stuff had been stressing her out since the day she'd received the meticulously calligraphed invitation requesting her presence at her little sister's nuptials. Throw in a couple of icy phone calls with her mother and a return-airfare-from-Seattle-to-Buffalo-shaped dent in her savings, and, well, Chloe was on the edge.

And people on the edge did stupid things, such as blub-

ber in front of a complete stranger, and then think dirty,
filthy thoughts about him. And while she'd found Ben
handsome from the start, something warm and wicked
was bubbling up to the surface now, waking parts of her
that had been dormant for…well, quite a while.

If not for the ring of the phone, she'd be letting Ben indulge a few of those parts right now. Suddenly the water
sluicing over her body felt hotter. She ran her soapy hands
over her breasts and across her stomach, the utilitarian
washing of her body growing sensual. She would love to
explore Ben's abs, to see if her brain had Photoshopped
them in hindsight, or if they were truly as spectacular
as she remembered. Her mind drifted lower and so did
her hands.

*Oh, God.*

She knew how long it had been since a man had
touched her—going on five months now—but how long
had it been since she'd touched herself? She couldn't remember the last time she'd indulged in the best stress
relief available to womankind.

Sure, nothing beat a willing partner, but there was
something to be said for being the one in control…of getting exactly what you wanted…right when you needed it.

*Yes. Oh, yes.*

Chloe reached out to brace her hand on the wall but
overshot and knocked the entire line of Value Inn mini
bath products off the built-in shelf. They rained down to
the tub with a series of bangs that jerked her out of the
moment. Her heartbeat, already revving from her sexy
daydreams, revved even higher with a shot of adrenaline.

Seriously? First the phone, and now this?

Chloe knew when she was beat. With a sigh, she
turned off the shower. She reached past the curtain to
pull one of the white hotel towels off the metal rack above

the toilet. Like all mass-laundered hotel towels, it was scratchy and barely reached the tops of her thighs when she wrapped it around herself.

The TV went silent as she stepped out of the tub. There were some muffled noises she couldn't quite place, and then the squeaky floor betrayed Ben's presence.

Chloe froze.

He was walking toward the bathroom.

Her hand flew to her chest, gripping the tiny towel in a tight fist. Her skin buzzed. Her heartbeat picked up. The light seeping under the bathroom door was interrupted by his shadow. There were only two inches of ramshackle door and a threadbare towel separating them. He was right…there…

"Chloe? You okay?"

Oh, man. His deep voice hit her right in the estrogen and her body picked up where it had left off in the shower. All that delicious heat flared back up. "Fine. Dropped something." The ability to form full sentences had deserted her.

"Okay. Well, good news. According to the weather forecast, the storm's moving quicker than they thought. It's already stopped snowing out there. We should get out of here on time tomorrow."

"Great." She hoped the word didn't come out as breathy as it had sounded to her own ears.

"I'm going to head downstairs and see a man about a cot. Or a woman. I'm not picky. Judging by the ominous 'no one's available to take your call' message I just got when I phoned the front desk, it might take a while. Wish me luck."

"Good luck." *Yep, pretty breathy*. Now she felt guilty for forming such a dark opinion of Stewardess Barbie.

Maybe the poor girl couldn't help it. Maybe it had been Ben's fault the whole time.

Then the hotel room door shrieked open and banged shut.

Chloe exhaled a shaky, disappointed breath.

What had she expected him to do? Bust open the door, profess their chemistry was undeniable, and ravish her like the hero in some old romance novel her grandma kept hidden at the back of her bookshelf? Well, kind of. But dudes got arrested for that kind of stuff nowadays.

With a sigh, Chloe wiped the steam from the mirror and stared at her blurry image.

Barefaced. Plain brown hair.

Maybe it was for the best that Ben hadn't broken down the door after all.

She barely recognized herself. She wasn't even in Buffalo yet and she was already reverting to the old Chloe. The one who'd been so desperate to escape. It was as if the closer she got to home, the more of her identity she was losing.

Her mother always said she wore too much makeup. It didn't matter how many strangers complimented her, or how many friends asked for a quick lesson. Her mother wouldn't be impressed that she'd worked her way from sales associate to manager of her local Titanium Beauty store in less than two years. Or that customers loved her makeup recommendations, and that the job afforded her a decent apartment and a means to pay her bills. To Fiona Masterson, it would never be more than a menial labor job at a makeup store in the mall.

And sure, her life wasn't as posh as her childhood had been, but she had a position in an industry she loved, and it was a great learning experience that was going to help her when she finally launched her own business and became a full-fledged makeup artist. She'd even started a YouTube channel where dozens of people thanked her for her tips and tricks on a weekly basis. It wasn't netting her much money yet, but she'd broken the five-hundred-dollar mark two months in a row. Not bad for a fledgling channel that relied on word of mouth.

Besides, making money wasn't the reason she had a YouTube channel. Mostly, it was a place for her to indulge her passion for makeup, for teaching women how to apply it, for investigating and reviewing products. Makeup wasn't just about vanity, it was about confidence, and she loved reading the comments of her subscribers as they discovered their best selves.

She grabbed the tiny blow-dryer that hung on the bathroom wall and attacked her wet hair with the renewed resolve of a woman with a plan. She was done feeling crappy about herself. She had a video to make for her regular Sunday night upload, anyway, so why not kill two birds with one stone?

First she was going to do her makeup.

Then she was going to do Ben.

## 3

Once her hair was under control, Chloe pulled on some sexy underwear—a black satin push-up bra with matching panties—and added a black T-shirt for modesty's sake. And socks.

Then she grabbed the cosmetic case and headed back into the room. She set her bag on the desk and liberated her laptop from her giant purse.

While it whirred to life at the touch of a button, Chloe took a seat and turned on the lamp beside her. She rummaged in her bag through the familiar jumble of eye shadow pots, Q-tips, brushes, eyeliners and mascara, making her selections as her computer booted up.

Once she'd settled on her makeup choices, she set to work, using the mirror hanging on the wall to make sure her concealer, foundation and powder were blended flawlessly into her skin. A little blush finished off her base, and she was ready for the fun stuff.

She went for a relatively simple daytime-appropriate look of blue-grays and soft purples.

Once she was happy with how her left eye had turned out, she pulled the laptop in front of her and opened the programs she needed. With the press of a button, her image appeared on the computer screen. She tucked her hair behind her ears and clicked Record.

"Hi, guys, Chloe here. I'm on the road this week, and as you can see," she motioned at the disheveled bed behind her, "my accommodations are not the most glamorous. But that's no reason not to look like a million bucks! So here's a quick makeup tutorial for all you jet-setters out there. A lot of you have been asking me for tips on what to bring with you on a trip. So my first recommendation is to pack a great eye shadow palette. With a palette, you get a lot of variety without taking up a lot of space, plus, all the colors are guaranteed to go together." She flipped the case full of blues and purples open and angled it toward the camera. "I'm going to be using this eye shadow palette by Jeweled Web—it's called Suburban Storm.

"For this look, I'm also going to be using an eyelash curler, my trusty brow gel, my favorite drugstore liquid liner, and the Lashes for Days mascara from Titanium Beauty." Chloe held each product up to the camera as she named it, and the routine of it all calmed her.

"As always, I've already done the left side, so you have an example of what we're aiming for." She turned her head a little and closed her eye. "So now that we've amassed the troops, I'll show you how to recreate this effect, and then we'll amp it up so you can see how an eye shadow palette can take you from business meeting to nightclub, even when you're away from home."

She fell easily into the rhythm of her makeup routine, chatting confidently at the camera, noticing from the corner of her eye that she was just approaching the five-minute mark as she finished up with her mascara wand. Perfect. Her under-six-minute videos always seemed to pull more views than the longer ones.

"So that's it." Chloe angled her head to the side, closed her eyes, opened them and leaned toward the laptop screen. "A dramatic look for a night out, or if you're like me, any given weekday. As always, if you have any questions, feel free to leave them in the comments. Thanks for watching. I'm Chloe and as I always say, 'makeup, not war'. Until next time."

Chloe clicked a few settings in the program, saved the video file, and set her laptop aside. Her weekly makeup tutorial was ready to post to her YouTube channel on Sunday night, as scheduled.

And she was ready for Ben.

BEN STOPPED IN front of the door and liberated the key card from his pocket, taking a moment to notice that his Prada dress shoes had fallen victim to the weather. The snow and salt had left streaks on the usually-gleaming black leather. He'd need to clean them before the big meeting tomorrow. The day he'd bought them, the salesgirl at the Bellevue Neiman Marcus had *oohed* and *aahed* over them, assuring him they were top-of-the-line, as comfortable as they were stylish, but if he was being honest, he still preferred the beat-up Converse shoes he used to wear.

*Dress for the job you want*, he reminded himself. It would all be worth it when he was hanging out at his cabin. He might even enforce a strict Chucks or barefeet-only policy there.

He unlocked the door and strode inside. "Chloe, they're out of cots, so…"

He stopped. Blinked. Tried to process the delectable sight before him.

"That's okay. I don't think we're going to need the cot, do you?"

"You're not wearing pants." It was an inane thing to say, but in his defense the blood was rushing away from his brain at an alarmingly fast rate.

Chloe's laugh was low and sexy. "You're a real charmer, Masterson, but your powers of observation are a little off," she chided, glancing down at herself, "because I'm— Oh, shit!" When she looked back at him, his seductress was frowning. "I meant to take the T-shirt off before you got back."

She reached for the hem and tugged her black shirt over her head, dropping it to the ground. Ben didn't think he'd ever been as deeply in lust with someone as he was with this woman in her sexy black-satin lingerie and a serviceable pair of black socks.

He wasn't sure if she'd awakened some weird sock fetish he'd never known he had, or if it was just damn adorable that she'd heeded his warning about cellulitis, but her brand of sensible sexuality had made him so hard it was a wonder his fly was still intact.

And that was before she walked over, grabbed him by the front of his shirt and kissed him like she'd been thinking about it at least as long as he had.

His arms came around her, pulling her closer. They both groaned at the full-body contact.

He kissed her again, licking into her mouth until he drew a sigh from her sweet pink lips. "You changed your makeup," he said, and the pleased expression on her face made him glad he'd mentioned it.

"I'm surprised you noticed."

"Well, in my defense, I'm a guy, so no pants trumps purple eye shadow every time. But that doesn't mean I won't get around to noticing how soft and pretty and touchable you look." He reached up and tucked her hair behind her ear. "So different than the badass green and black from earlier."

She tightened her grip on his neck, pulling him down for another kiss, and they were both panting when their lips parted again.

"I've wanted this since the moment we shook hands on the plane," he confessed, kissing her jaw and running his fingers over smooth, warm skin and cool black satin.

"That's pretty presumptuous, Masterson." Despite her words, she tipped her head back so he could continue trailing kisses down her neck. He walked her backward to the bed.

"How is it presumptuous?"

"I just decided this was going to happen while I was in the shower. Sex definitely wasn't on the table before that."

"Sure it was," he countered, placing her on the mattress. "Ask Spider."

Chloe's laugh was full and rich as she scooted up on the bed so she could recline on the pillows. "I can't believe you just said that! I share my tragic past with you and you use it against me?"

He pulled off her socks. "Face it, Chloe. This was meant to be. The plane? The hotel mix-up? Fate's practically begging us to have sex."

Her smile was decadent. "I think you may have misunderstood the difference between fate and hormones."

"No way. This is definitely fate." Ben joined her on the bed. "I mean they don't call it a *layover* for nothing."

"Stop that," she said with a breathy giggle that drove him wild. Ben was enchanted, no doubt about it. And very turned on. "Stop what?"

"Stop making me laugh."

He kissed her collarbone. "Why?"

"Because one-night stands aren't supposed to be funny, they're supposed to be torrid and sexy and raw."

"Oh, I can do torrid."

COULD HE EVER.

His expression darkened seconds before he caught her mouth in a scorching, wet kiss that convinced her they were both wearing way too many clothes.

She reached for the buttons on his dress shirt, fumbling them open with lust-clumsy fingers. When she'd finally popped the last one, he rewarded her with a shift of his hips that brought their bodies into perfect alignment, and the pleasure that streaked through her made her gasp.

*Damn* he felt good. Hot and hard. Her fingers curled against his skin, and her hips bucked to get closer. He groaned, grinding harder against her, squeezing her breast with a large, warm hand. She wanted Ben, naked and panting, thrusting inside her until she couldn't think, couldn't breathe.

She couldn't care less about her mother's disappointment, or her sister's wedding, or her exile in Chicago.

She felt alive. And sexy. And desperate for more.

She ran her palms across his beautiful shoulders and down his back. When she reached the waistband of his pants, she let her fingers follow the material around to his stomach and traced the reverse path, up his ridged abdomen and hair-roughened chest.

"Oh, God," he rasped, pulling away a little, but she rose up, catching his mouth as she ran a thumb across his nipple, delighting in the shudder that quaked through him at her touch. "Chloe, stop for a second."

"Make me," she growled playfully, nipping his bottom lip, loving the way his muscles jumped at her touch. He groaned. "*Jesus*, you feel so good." He kissed her back, hot and frantic, before tearing his mouth away again.

"Chloe, are you sure about this?"

Ben was staring down at her, hair mussed, eyes dark, looking like the answer to all her sexual frustrations. "I need this, Ben." She was desperate to experience more of the buzzing current running between them, to block out the shitty stuff and lose herself with this man.

She might as well have said *abracadabra*, her words had such a magical effect on him. That last little bit of concern that had lingered disappeared in a wolfish grin. "I meant are you sure about the bed," he lied. "Because I'd be happy to move this over to the table if you want to be able to tell a better story at the stagette."

"I already missed the stagette," she responded, pressing a kiss against his jaw, "and the family brunch," she kissed his neck, "the reception for out-of-town guests," the hollow of his throat, "the rehearsal," his collarbone, "the rehearsal dinner—"

"Oh, okay, now who's being funny? This bed is a joke-free zone, Masterson. Your rule, not mine."

"You're right," she conceded. She leaned back and raised an eyebrow. "You'd better take off your clothes and get me on track again."

His mouth hitched up at the corner in a devilish half smile. "Yeah, baby. I got your torrid right here," he said, and her laughter betrayed her change of heart. Maybe *funny* did have its place in the bedroom after all.

Ben got to his feet and pulled his shirt the rest of the way off.

She'd never been into male strippers—way too cheesy for her taste—but watching Ben strip was a study in seduction. There was no teasing or coyness, just a man taking off his clothes.

And then, finally, he stood naked and aroused in front of her. All sinewy muscle and powerful limbs. And she wanted him. All of him.

"Your turn," he said, his voice so low and raspy that she shivered.

Chloe pushed onto her knees, reaching behind her back to unhook her bra. She peeled the material away slowly and air rushed against her skin, doing nothing to cool the heat that raged inside her.

Then there was nothing left between them but her underwear. She tucked her thumbs into the waistband, inching them down her thighs. It was one of the sexiest moments of her life, revealing herself to him this way, and his predatory stare raised goose bumps on her skin.

"You're so beautiful."

And she believed him in that moment because she felt beautiful. Powerful. Tonight she was daring and sexy, an erotic fantasy. With a grin that was pure siren, she slipped her panties off the rest of the way and tossed them to the floor. "So what are you going to do about it?"

"Oh, I've got a couple of ideas," he promised with a wicked smile. He grabbed protection from somewhere inside his suitcase. Chloe kept her eyes on him as he ripped into the package. She was surprised by how sexy it was, watching him handle himself, roll the condom down the length of his shaft.

She'd never really paid much attention to this part of the process before. She was usually too far inside her own head—How did she look? How did he think she looked? How could she make her boobs seem bigger and her stomach seem flatter?—to pay much attention.

She was paying attention now.

He was big, deliciously so.

She was all damp heat and wanting. When she licked

her lips, he practically pounced on her, pressing her back into the mattress. Then he shifted and his erection was between her legs and it was so perfect having him there, just where she wanted him.

When he started circling his hips, applying more pressure, Chloe nearly cried out. "Deeper," she whispered, burying her head in the crook of his neck. "Please."

He was inside her with a single thrust, a fast, hard invasion of her body that knocked the wind from her in the best possible way.

"I want you so much, Chloe," he growled, proving it with every flex of his hips, until she was wild beneath him—panting, sweating, clinging.

Her body was on fire for him. She pulled her knees up, trying to get closer, and the slight change in position must've felt just as good to him as it did to her, because he swore and upped his pace. Her entire world had narrowed to the pressure building inside her.

Suddenly, he pushed himself up on one elbow, but before Chloe had a chance to mourn the loss of his chest against her breasts, he moved his hand between them and rubbed his thumb roughly against the most sensitive part of her, startling a cry from her throat. Her brain short-circuited as a sharp shock of white-hot heat rolled through her, swamping her with pleasure a moment before he joined her in nirvana.

# *4*

BEN STEPPED FROM the jet bridge onto the plane, stifling a yawn. He was definitely feeling the lack of sleep. Not that he was complaining. The mere memory of Chloe writhing beneath him, his hands on her skin, her tongue in his mouth... Ben shifted with discomfort as his dick stirred at the erotic recollection.

What he *planned* to complain about when he saw Chloe again was the fact that he'd woken up alone this morning. But first he had to make it to his seat. He shuffled farther into the plane, waiting as the gentleman in front of him hoisted his suitcase into the overhead compartment.

Jesus, he could still *smell* her. It was an unfortunate by-product of an overactive imagination and this morning's shower. He'd used what she'd left in the tiny bottle of complimentary hotel shampoo, and now the achingly familiar perfume of flowers lingered around him. Normally it would have made him nauseous, but thanks to the wrestling match on the bed last night, it was making him horny.

Ben pushed a hand through his Chloe-scented hair and continued to sidestep down the narrow aisle until he arrived at row G and the object of his lust-filled fantasies came into view.

She was wearing faded jeans and a white T-shirt with a zombified Audrey Hepburn on it. Her lips were stained a deep shade of berry; her eyeliner was back with gothic vengeance. And if his cock had been mildly interested at the memory of her, the reality of Chloe had its full attention.

*Her* attention, though, was studiously focused on the in-flight magazine in her lap.

"Is this seat taken?"

She glanced up as he shoved his carry-on into the overhead bin. She might have sighed as he brushed past her to sit down, but he couldn't be sure.

"Guess I should have thought this through a little better. I was trying for a dramatic and mysterious exit after a single night of passion." She flipped a glossy page with her index finger.

"Yeah, assigned seating really messes with drama."

She flipped another page. "Worst one-night-stand exit ever."

"On the contrary. You were very quiet when you left— I didn't wake up at all. Nothing was drawn on my face in permanent marker, and I still have my watch, my wallet and my credit cards," Ben countered charitably. "As far as I'm concerned, this ranks very high on the scale."

His joke earned him a withering glare.

"I meant that we're stuck in forced proximity and tight confines, with no choice but to ignore each other awkwardly and try to keep our arms from touching until we can finally go our separate ways. Which reminds me, I'm claiming this now." She laid her right arm on the armrest from elbow to wrist, completely covering it from view.

"Or...we could defy the expected and skip the awkward silence. Just keep on living life as though I didn't ruin you for other men last night."

She raised an unimpressed eyebrow.

"Look, Chloe. We've got about an hour of forced proximity left to go here. So what do you say we move on, start over?"

"START OVER?" she asked speculatively. *Like I'm not completely and utterly mortified that I jumped you in the hotel room last night?* "As in we do that lame handshake thing in all the girly movies and reintroduce ourselves?"

Ben laughed, and the rumbling sound put a dent in her defenses. "Yeah, that."

With a shrug of acquiescence, Chloe held her hand out. "I'm Latoya."

Ben smirked at her as they shook. "Julio."

"Hmm. Sexy name. So tell me, Julio, what do you do for a living?"

She was expecting a smart-ass comment, like "romance novel cover model," but instead she got: "What do you *think* I do?"

She arched her right eyebrow. "Honestly?"

He nodded.

"Sales." She didn't even hesitate. "Ad exec, maybe? That or hocking used cars."

"Wow. Don't take a second to think about it or anything." Ben's voice was light, jokey, but his forehead was a bit furrowed, and there was a gravitas to his next words. "How come?"

"Are you kidding me?"

His silence said he was not.

She gave a one-shouldered shrug. "I don't know. The way you dress is part of it." She eyed his attire.

"Lots of men wear suits. Newscasters. Athletes. Mob bosses. The alter-egos of superheroes."

She remained unmoved. "Am I right?"

Ben shrugged. "I can neither confirm nor deny this line of questioning until you tell me what you do."

"What do you *think* I do?" she mimicked.

He turned in his seat to look at her, *really* look at her, and Chloe squirmed a little under the inspection. She was *this close* to blushing. To counteract the uncomfortable feeling, she forced herself to square her shoulders and raise her chin a notch.

"Well, I'm gonna strike flight attendant and used car salesman from the list of possibilities, considering your obvious scorn for those professions."

Chloe flashed him a tight smile. *Ha, ha.*

"Um, okay. You're *not* a dentist. You're *not* the vice president of anything." His eyes darted to the zombie on her T-shirt. "And you're *not* a kindergarten teacher."

She narrowed her eyes. "Why do I suddenly feel like this game is going to be less than flattering?"

"What do you mean, *suddenly*? Did you *hear* the way you say *sales*?"

"Just guess already," she urged, but with a sinking sensation in her stomach. Chloe wasn't so sure that she wanted to know Ben's impressions of her.

"I think you're an artist."

Her eyebrows shot up in surprise.

He nodded slowly, contemplatively. "Whatever you do, it's something that other people only wish they did. I bet you illustrate comic books, or sing in a band, or create amazing sculptures out of ordinary, everyday things." He squinted at her, analyzing. "There's a slight chance you're a little more corporate about it, though—like a graphic designer, or maybe you have a clothing line in the works."

Chloe sucked in her breath. It was highly possible that that was the nicest thing anyone had ever said about her. Or *to* her, for that matter.

"So? Am I close?"

God, that lopsided grin was adorable.

In a really weird way that she refused to scrutinize, Chloe didn't want to disappoint him with the truth. Or herself. What was the point of squashing the warmth in her chest with cold, bitter reality? She liked the way Ben saw her, full of possibilities. She wasn't ready to relinquish that feeling yet.

"You know what, Ben? You and I are going to return to our regularly scheduled lives in just over an hour, right?"

He glanced at his watch. "Thereabouts."

"So how about we don't ruin today with anything as mundane as the truth? I mean, think about it. In your lifetime, how many people have you spent the night with who didn't know what you did for a living?"

Ben's lips quirked in a bit of a smile. "None."

"Exactly. So let's not label ourselves. Let's embrace that rebellious streak of yours, Mr. Lone Wolf. Let's live dangerously and talk to strangers."

"Huh. Impassioned speech. Is this your way of keeping me from guessing your true occupation? Because if you're a politician, I promise I won't think less of you," he vowed.

Chloe relaxed in her seat and let the hour fly by, literally and figuratively, as she talked to Ben.

CHLOE STOOD NEXT to Ben, watching the unfamiliar luggage circling past them on the conveyer belt.

After they'd decided not to make the usual small talk about themselves, they'd ended up bonding over innocuous things like a mutual hatred of sunglasses that rivaled dinner plates in circumference, and a shared belief that specialty cartoon channels had massacred the joy of childhood Saturday mornings.

Turned out Ben was just as cool as she'd suspected. It would figure she'd spent the past four years dating nothing but losers, only to run into one of the good ones when she was only looking for a one-night stand.

"The boutonnieres are an absolute disgrace. How will it look with the groomsmen wearing champagne roses when the rest of the wedding flowers are white?"

*Oh no.* Chloe turned toward the familiar voice growing ever louder as a woman with a cell phone to her ear barked orders and stalked toward the baggage claim. Not even the bustle of an international airport could mute this particular woman scorned.

"We're not going to pay for this kind of lack of attention on your part. That's right. Yes, eight new boutonnieres made with white roses. We'll be expecting them by noon. Yes, that's the correct address. Tell the concierge it's for the Masterson–Van Allen wedding."

Ignoring Ben's questioning look, Chloe took off toward her mother, trying to keep as much distance between him and Fiona Masterson as possible. No need to complicate things any more than they already were.

"Mom! Hi." The second the words were out of her mouth, four years of distance swirled up around them and stole Chloe's breath. Her mother looked the same. A little older, obviously, but as regal as ever.

Her graying hair was pulled back into the elegant chignon she favored. She was dressed in black from head to toe, all designer labels, all tailored to perfection for her slim frame. Even the posh winter coat. Her jewellery was gold, but her earrings were pearls. The first piece of jewelry Chloe's father had ever given her, the night he'd professed his love, a mere seven dates into their courtship. That's what her mother had always called it, their "courtship". As a little girl the tale had been one of Chloe's favorite bedtime stories, and she would beg her mother to tell it night after night.

And now they were reduced to exchanging an awkward air kiss in an airport terminal.

"Chloe Marie, it's about time you got here." Her mother made a production of glancing around as she dropped her phone into her Louis Vuitton handbag. "Alone, I see. That's going to throw off the seating chart. You couldn't have RSVP'd to let us know so that we could rearrange the tables earlier, I suppose. I'm sure selling makeup to mall patrons keeps you from picking up the phone. Never mind that an uneven seating chart can completely derail a wedding."

Chloe gritted her teeth in her best semblance of a smile. "What are you doing here? We agreed to meet at the hotel."

"I was ironing out a few last-minute things for the wedding, so I had the car service bring me here. I thought you could come back to the bridal suite with me. You can get ready there, so I don't have to worry about you being late for tonight's ceremony. Also, I need someone to keep an eye on your sister while I check on the catering staff. You know they…"

Her mother's eyes widened and the rest of the chastisement died on her lips a split second before an arm slipped around Chloe's waist.

"I've got our bags, babe. Mrs. Masterson, it's great to

finally meet you. I'm Ben." He extended a hand in Fiona Masterson's direction, and Chloe could only mirror her mother's shocked expression as he delivered the coup de grâce. "Chloe's boyfriend."

# 5

IT WASN'T ON PURPOSE. He wasn't a knight in shining armor. But something about seeing this smart-mouthed goddess who'd rocked-and-socked her way into his world fade into a shadow of herself was disheartening.

He liked Chloe. She was funny and jaded, but not quite as jaded as she thought she was. Their conversations over the past twelve hours had been the most fun he'd had with a woman in a really long time. And had he mentioned the sex had been hot as hell? Truly top-notch. So why bring the fun to an end?

Besides, it wasn't like he had plans tonight. His meeting with hotel magnate Edward Burke was at four o'clock. By five he'd be free and clear. And a guy had to eat, so what did he care if it was room service or fancy wedding food?

"I'm sorry, what did you say your name was again?"

"Ben, ma'am."

"Ben. Is that short for Benjamin?"

"It is."

"May I call you Benjamin?"

"Of course."

She finally accepted his outstretched hand, eyeing

him coolly. He felt every second of her assessment, like her eyes were shooting tiny, prickling ice shards as they studied him. His face, his suit, his arm around her daughter's waist, his shoes. He was glad he'd taken the time to polish them that morning. "It's nice to meet you, Benjamin. Chloe failed to mention she was seeing a handsome professional man. What is it that you do for a living?"

"Mom! Boundaries. Geez."

"Fine. We'll talk about it in the car on the way to the suite."

Ben put on his best client-wooing smile. "I really appreciate the offer, Mrs. Masterson—"

"Fiona," she corrected.

"Fiona. But I've got a business meeting this afternoon, so we should really head straight to our room."

"Yes, Ben's got a meeting first!" Chloe latched onto the excuse with all her might. "He can't be late for that. So…yeah, what Ben said. Gotta get to our hotel. Check in and stuff."

"Hotel Burke," Ben added, hoping the ritzy name would impress Chloe's mom a little, or at least thaw her a bit. She didn't bat an eye. Chloe groaned.

"Well, I'm relieved to hear you're staying at the wedding venue. I figured you would have picked something clear across the city, just to be contrary."

"See you tonight, Mom." Chloe reached for her luggage, but Ben beat her to it, grabbing her scratched-up plastic suitcase in his left hand, his pristine black one in his right. "I got it."

"What the hell was that?" Chloe whirled on him the second they stepped outside. The frigid wind whipped her hair around her head, and Ben set their suitcases down on the snowy sidewalk so he could shove his hands in his pockets.

"Unbalanced seating plans are wedding kryptonite."

"Oh, God. You heard that?"

Ben shrugged his shoulders against the cold. "It's a well-known fact. I can't believe you weren't aware of it, Chloe Marie."

"I can't believe you told her you're my boyfriend." Chloe jammed a hand through her hair. "Why would you do that?"

"I believe the words you're looking for are 'thank you, Ben.'"

"Why would I thank you? You've ruined everything!"

"What are you talking about? I just saved your ass."

"In what world did you save me? Now I'm going to get a lecture three times as embarrassing as before because she won't have a chance to even out the damn seating arrangement before I arrive solo at the big event." She pulled her coat tighter around her. "Maybe I could just say you got hit by a bus, or you're allergic to tulle—"

"Or I could just come with."

"—or you ate some bad shellfish or— What?"

"What time does it start?"

Chloe stared up at him with no sign of understanding on her face. The tip of her nose was turning pink in the cold.

"The wedding," he clarified.

"I, uh, let me check."

"You don't even know when the ceremony starts? Isn't that like, the raison d'être of bridesmaids?"

She fished a thick, pearlescent envelope from the depths of her purse. "Oh, I'm not a bridesmaid," she told him, pulling a fancy-looking itinerary out of the envelope.

Ben's shoulders drooped. As an only child with no

living family, he'd kind of romanticized the idea of having blood relatives. Chloe's words shook him a little.

"According to this, the ceremony starts at six, appetizers and cocktails are at seven, late supper and speeches start at eight."

"Perfect. My meeting should be done by five at the latest. Gives me a chance to shower and change."

She stared up at him again, this time with skepticism. "You sure you want to do this, Masterson?"

"You underestimate the things I will do for a free dinner, Chloe Marie. Now c'mon. Let's grab a taxi before I lose my ears to frostbite."

THE VALUE INN had been adequate. Hotel Burke was spectacular. Vaulted ceilings, glittering chandeliers, sumptuous fabrics, and rich wood lent the place an air of old-world glamour.

Ben gave a low, impressed whistle. "So your mom takes a car service and your sister's getting hitched *here*? What's the deal? You're actually some poor little rich girl or something?"

"My parents have money. I don't have money."

He'd been teasing, but something in her voice caught his attention. She'd gone very still.

"Hey, I was just teasing."

She smiled to reassure him, but didn't quite pull it off. "I know. It's no big deal. I'm just... I'd kind of forgotten what this was all like, this life I left behind."

Growing up with just his dad who'd often struggled to make ends meet, he couldn't quite imagine anyone walking away from all this and being fine with it. It was the dream, what most people strove for. "Do you regret it?"

She shook her head, pretty green eyes darting around the ornate lobby. "No. I mean, in the big picture, there's no difference between the Value Inn and this place. A hotel is just a place to sleep, right? But it reminds me of the person I used to be."

Her hand drifted subconsciously to her hair. *Boring old brown*, she'd called it. He wondered what she was remembering as emotions flitted across her face—sad eyes, a ghost of a smile, the determined set of her chin.

The desire to pry was overwhelming. He wanted to learn everything there was to learn about the beautiful, complicated woman beside him. But right now she needed to be distracted.

"Shall we go check in?"

"Huh? Oh. Um, yeah. About that…"

He turned to face her.

"You know what my mom said? About me booking a room across town just to be contrary?"

The guilty look on her face made him smile. "Seriously?"

She nodded sheepishly.

"Stay with me."

Chloe's cheeks bloomed with color. "What?"

"I like you," Ben confessed. "The real you. But you're different when you're around your mom. And I get it," he hurried to explain himself, "because I've had people in my life like that, too. People you can't quite be yourself with." Melanie's face came to mind, right on cue, but Ben was surprised that his bosses' faces were also part of the mental parade.

"Thanks, Ben. That's really nice of you, but…"

*Uh-oh.* He'd spooked her. He should've known better. Chloe preferred to keep things light.

To that end, he lowered his voice and leaned in closer. "Also I really enjoy getting you naked. So what do you say? How about we make this a two-night stand?"

Her smile told him he'd saved the mission. Well, him and the fact she didn't have much choice now that her mother thought she'd be staying here. "Why, Mr. Masterson, are you suggesting what I think you're suggesting?"

"I really hope so." God, did he hope so.

"I'm in, but only if you let me pay half," she stipulated, "because I don't want the guy at the desk to label me a hooker."

"I accept your terms, because the room's actually a comp. When you do business with Edward Burke, you stay free at his hotel. And for the record, there's no way anyone working at a classy place like this would ever mistake you for a common hooker. This is call-girl territory."

"Well, in that case," she teased, grabbing his hand, "hurry up and get us a room already."

The man behind the counter was extremely efficient and they were in the elevator and headed up to their room in no time.

Smiling and laughing, bumping into each other more than was strictly necessary, the low-grade sexual tension that had been simmering between them escalated the closer they got to the room. He loved this playful side of her.

"Look at this place." Ben held the door open so Chloe could join him in the tiled foyer. A freakin' *foyer*, with a shoe rack, and a closet, and a giant urn full of fake palm-fronds. The room was stunning, done in opulent shades of brown and cream. "And this isn't even a suite."

"Forget the foyer, I'm more interested in checking out the bed. You wanna help me with the inspection?" The wheels of her suitcase were quieted as they met carpet when she ventured farther into the room.

"Oh, hell yes." Ben pushed the door closed behind

them and locked the bar latch as he glanced at the emergency map.

*In case of fire, use stairs unless otherwise instructed.*

"Ben? Are you coming? Because I want to."

*Notify the operator (dial 0) or pull nearest fire alarm.*

"Nothing? That was a grade A pun, Masterson. Right up there with 'Mrs. Understanding.'"

*If you hear the fire alarm, evacuate, don't investigate.*

"Are you seriously reading about the fire escape routes?" Her voice was so close it startled him, and he spun to face her, embarrassed at being caught.

"It's just good sense to know where the closest emergency exits and fire extinguishers are."

She shook her head at him in faux disappointment. "You're such a freak sometimes, Masterson."

"Uh, yeah. A freak in the sack."

"Prove it," she challenged, squealing in surprise as he wrapped his arms around her and hoisted her up his body. She wrapped her legs around his waist and kissed him back as he carried her over to the bed before dropping her unceremoniously on the giant mattress.

"With pleasure," he said, divesting himself of his suit jacket and shoes.

"Ooh, I like the sound of that." She reached up, pulling his tie down until he joined her on the bed. He pushed her down onto the pillows.

Then he settled beside her, propping himself on his elbows so he could stare down at her. Her makeup was different again. Today his little chameleon was sporting a clever blend of pinks and browns that made the golden flecks in her green eyes shine.

She raised her hand to his cheek, startling him out of his inspection, and he accepted her wordless invitation and lowered his lips to hers.

The soft meeting of their mouths was a revelation, so different than the last time she'd been in his arms. That had been the heat and passion of a match meeting gasoline. This was a slow burn, and he let himself revel in the sweet eroticism, the simple beauty of just kissing her.

The first sweep of her tongue made his breath catch. As much as he loved the soft brush of her lips on his, tasting, teasing, he was relieved as the pressure built because he was starting to go out of his mind with all this restraint. His breath came faster, his mouth grew more demanding, and he ached to touch Chloe everywhere.

She pressed her palm to his chest, curling her fingers into his shirt, tugging him closer. He loved knowing she was as turned on by their make-out session as he was. She had just started in on his shirt buttons when the shrill ring of her cell phone intruded on the moment.

He rested his forehead against hers. "Ignore it."

"It's my mom. She'll only call back if I don't answer. Again and again and again. Trust me. It's why I assigned her a special ringtone in the first place."

With a sigh, Ben flopped onto his back as she crawled across the bed in search of her phone. It took a moment of digging through her purse and four more rings to answer the call.

"Hi, Mom…Yes, we're here…" She glanced over at Ben, rolling her eyes. "Right now?…Okay, I'll be there in a minute…Yes, the fourth floor…I understand that you're on seven, and I know how to use an elevator, so I'm sure this will all work out fine. Okay…Okay…Yes… Mom, I'm coming right up…I'm coming right up! We can talk about it when I get there. I'll see you in a minute."

"What, did she follow our cab to make sure we came straight here?"

"I wouldn't put it past her." Chloe tugged her T-shirt

back into place as she stood. "I am really sorry about this. But I'm glad you're coming to this wedding with me. I don't know how I'd have gotten through this by myself, so thank you."

He stacked his hands behind his head and waggled his eyebrows. "You can thank me later."

God, he loved making her laugh.

"I really wish I didn't have to leave." She walked over to the mirror and fussed a little with her hair. "I have no idea how long this will take, so good luck with your meeting."

"You can good luck me later, too."

She turned and hit him with a sultry look that upped the heat simmering in his belly. "Oh, I'll luck you all right." She started walking toward him with a slinky, do-me walk that drove him crazy. "And it's gonna be so good," she promised, leaning over to plant a final kiss on his mouth. Ben grabbed her around the waist and pulled her down on top of him.

She giggled against his lips, squirming to get back up. "Ben, I have to go or she'll send out a search party!"

He groaned as she got free of his embrace and pushed herself up off the bed.

"Fiona Masterson waits for no woman."

"Fine," he relented. "Get out of here already. I have a meeting to prepare for."

"I'll see you back here when I'm done." She grabbed a tube of lipstick from her purse and did a quick touch-up before heading for the door.

"Hey, Chloe?"

She glanced over her shoulder at him.

"Bet you wish you knew where all the emergency exits were now, huh?"

She was still laughing when she pulled the door shut behind her.

CHLOE TRIED TO control her grin as she approached the bridal suite, but it just kept slipping out. It had been a long time since she'd liked a man this much. And really, this was the perfect situation for her. A two-night stand. A vacation fling—no commitments, no expectations, just fun, flirting, and—

"There you are, Chloe! I've got to get down to the ballroom to make sure it's ready. Please go and keep your sister company." Chloe accepted the key card her mother held out to her. "She's all alone in there—talking some nonsense about needing a minute to herself."

"Well, we can't have that."

"Exactly." The word was so emphatic that Chloe almost laughed, until she realized the reason for her mother's panic. It had very little to do with Caroline, and everything to do with a Saturday afternoon four years ago. The insight sobered her. "I'll sit with her. Go take care of the catering."

With a deep breath, Chloe unlocked the door to the massive bridal suite and stepped inside. Her sister was dressed in a white-satin robe with her brown hair pinned and curled into an elaborate updo. She was sitting at a mirrored vanity, looking beautiful and vulnerable, like some old-timey movie star.

"Mom, I'm fine. I promise. I just… Chloe! You made it."

Caroline was so different than Chloe remembered, and it was more than the fancy hair and lack of makeup. Sure, they were friends on Facebook—she'd seen her little sister mugging for the camera in internet pictures, but they didn't convey Caroline's presence, her stillness. She seemed so grown up for twenty. Well, twenty-one.

"Happy birthday."

"Thanks, Chlo."

Chloe was surprised by the nickname. A remnant from grade school, when having matching four-letter nicknames that ended with *O* was the height of sisterly bonding—back when they used to get along. Caro and Chlo. It all seemed a lifetime ago.

"And thank you for coming. When Mom said your flight was delayed, I was worried you might not make it."

Her sister's sincerity made Chloe feel a little bad for not wanting to come.

"I know we haven't seen each other for ages, but I need your help."

Chloe laughed nervously. "Don't you have a half-dozen bridesmaids around to do your bidding? Where is everyone?"

"They'll be here soon. They're just finishing up in hair and makeup in the suite next door. I just wanted a few minutes to myself. Today's been flying by so fast I feel like I haven't had a moment to breathe. Besides, I didn't want them around when I asked you."

"Asked me what?"

Caroline bit her lip, an old nervous habit. "Would you do my makeup?"

The question stopped Chloe dead. "What?"

"I want you to do my makeup. Like old times."

She used to practice on Caroline constantly. At first, she'd done it against her little sister's will, bribing her to play guinea pig with sweets or toys or money. Then later, she'd done it at Caroline's behest, for dances and dates and parties. But all that had been many years ago.

"You want… I mean, didn't you hire a professional makeup artist?"

"You're a professional makeup artist. That's what you do at work, right? And on YouTube?"

Chloe blinked. "You've seen my videos?"

"Of course! And don't try to wuss out on me and say you don't have your stuff, because I'm sure that giant purse of yours is full of every color and cosmetic known to man."

It was true, so Chloe didn't bother to deny it.

"You're sure?"

At Caroline's nod, she walked over and set her purse on the vanity, ignoring the way her sister's eyes lit up as she began unpacking her stuff.

Chloe's hand was shaking as she pumped some foundation onto a makeup sponge, and she forced herself to take a deep breath to still the tremor. She was just about to start the application when Caroline held out her hand to stop her.

Chloe raised her eyebrows.

"Listen, you're not going to do my makeup exactly the way you do yours, right? I mean, you won't use green or anything? And less eyeliner, okay? I'm not going to a rock concert. I'm getting married."

Chloe laughed at that, and the overwhelming tension that had been tying knots into her shoulders since she'd stepped in the room lessened. "Shut up and trust me, brat."

Caroline smiled and did just that.

Twenty minutes later, Chloe was pretty damn impressed with her handiwork. Her sister was glowing in soft shades of nudes and pinks, looking every inch the blushing bride. A second coat of mascara and she'd be ready for her big moment.

Chloe twisted the cap off the tube and leaned in to apply the finishing touch.

"I wanted to ask you to be a bridesmaid."

Chloe's hand jerked at the admission, and the brush touched her sister's eyebrow. "Oh, God. Hold on, I can fix that!" She jammed the wand back into the tube with undue haste and started digging through her bag for her makeup remover. She didn't notice her hands were shaking until Caroline touched her forearm and she froze.

"Don't worry about the mascara." The soft, understanding note in her sister's voice gave Chloe the courage to look at her. "I just wanted you to know that I wanted you here."

Why was it hard to breathe?

"Mom kyboshed the bridesmaid idea pretty quick, I'm sure." She was joking, so she hoped Caroline had missed the note of hurt that stained the words.

Her little sister shook her head, staring at her lap. "I—I decided not to ask you." Caroline looked up, and once again, Chloe saw the woman she'd grown into. Nothing like the spoiled brat of her memories. "I figured the only way I'd get you here was to make you as anonymous as possible."

"Really good guess," Chloe managed to say.

"I needed you to be part of this, Chloe. I miss you. I know we didn't used to get along well, but I was a stupid teenager. I was jealous of my big sister, the rebel! Doing what she wanted, being who she wanted. And then you just left," she said, voice trembling.

"Oh, God, don't cry. You'll ruin your makeup," Chloe warned, but they were both far past being able to obey.

"I'm sure you've always thought of me as a goody two-shoes, doing what Mom and Dad wanted. And a lot of the time, you were right. I was. But not today. I'm not getting married to show you up. Or because Mom is friends with his mother. I don't care that he's going to be a doctor. I love Dalton. I love him and he loves me. I just wanted to tell you that. I'm going to be Mrs. Van Allen because I want to be."

Chloe nodded, grabbing a tissue from the vanity for her sister, and one for herself. "I'm happy for you, Caro." They both daubed under their eyes for stray tears. "Now stop bawling and let's fix your face."

A cotton swab's worth of makeup remover and a few more swipes of mascara, and Caroline looked perfectly perfect.

"Oh, my gosh, Chloe. This is amazing! I never... I never thought I could look like this. I'm blown away."

There was a knock on the door a moment before six girls in matching ice-blue dresses came rushing in, chattering like happy little birds, oohing and aahing over the beautiful bride.

That was her cue to leave. Chloe shoved all her stuff back in her bag, and headed for the door. She managed to catch her sister's eye through the crowd, and gave her a nod. Caroline managed a little wave before being swept toward the massive white garment bag hanging beside the window.

So far, today had not turned out anything like she'd expected. And as she stepped into the hallway, Chloe could honestly say that she'd never been happier to be wrong.

BEN STEPPED INTO Edward Burke's richly-furnished office and adjusted his suit jacket. As he mentally reviewed his pitch, he drummed a beat against his thigh and took in his surroundings.

You could tell a lot about a client by where they held their business meetings. Unlike the chrome-and-glass austerity of the Carson and McLeod offices, Burke's home base was a blend of warm colors, dark wood and surprising homey touches—he'd lay bets the colorful

Afghan blankets that hung on the backs of the leather visitors' chairs were hand-knit.

Ben sauntered over to the far wall and was perusing the framed crayon drawings that hung there when Burke entered the suite. He pointed at the art. "Early Picasso?"

Burke smiled, drawing Ben's attention to his bushy white mustache. "Picasso would have sold his soul to be as prolific as my grandkids."

Ben shook his proffered hand.

"Mr. Masterson, it's nice to finally meet you in person. Take a seat."

"Call me Ben, please," he insisted, accepting the offer to sit. "It's an honor to be in the room with you as well, sir."

Burke undid the button on his brown tweed suit jacket before he took a seat behind his desk. He pushed a folder full of papers toward Ben. Judging from the bits he could see, many of them sported the gray-and-black Carson and McLeod letterhead.

"Frankly, Ben, I'm a little surprised you're here. I was expecting the firm to send a family man to try to pull the wool over my eyes—someone who could better understand my brand."

*Guess the niceties are over.* "Mr. Burke, I assure you, I am the man for this job."

"I'm not denying that you're talented. Your campaigns are catchy, memorable and well put together. But they've all targeted young, single men. Hotel Burke is a luxury experience for the whole family. Traditional, not trendy."

"I understand your concerns. But I've done massive amounts of research in preparation for this meeting. I know what you're looking for, and I wouldn't have flown all the way here if I didn't believe I could deliver it. Carson and McLeod will take Hotel Burke to the next level."

There it was. That jolt, the excitement that came from figuring out a client, not what they wanted, but what they needed—and being confident that he was the one who could help them get it. *This*. This moment was the part of the job Ben loved. The rest was all white noise.

"I understand that tradition is important to you. It's obvious from the way you run your brand and the way you live your life. But as important as the past is, you have to ensure your future, as well. It's crucial that you reach the next generation of Hotel Burke guests. Let me show you what I've got in mind..."

THE ROOM WAS empty when she got back, and Chloe used the opportunity to shower and dry her hair. For the wedding, she livened up her brown bob with some messy, rocker-chick curls. She also decided to forgo her usual smoky eye for something a little less dramatic. If her sister wanted less eyeliner, Chloe figured she could handle that for one night.

"Chloe?"

"In here," she called, and Ben stuck his head into the bathroom.

"Hey. You're back! And your hair looks amazing." He held up the garment bag slung over his shoulder. "Got my suit pressed, so I just need to jump in the shower and I'll be ready to go."

"Okay. I'm almost done in here." She grabbed a tube of lipstick and painted her lips a deep, luscious red.

There was something intimate and domestic about getting ready with a man—having him ducking in and out, hanging up his suit and laying out his shoes and socks as she put the final touches on her makeup.

"Okay, all yours," she announced.

Ben pressed a kiss to her forehead as they traded

spaces, and as Chloe stepped back into the room to finish getting ready, she found she was feeling pretty optimistic. Like maybe she was going to make it through this wedding after all.

By the time she'd pulled on her dress and buckled up her shoes, though, she wasn't so sure. Her reunion with Caroline might have exceeded expectations, but the hard part was still ahead of her.

The shower had gone silent, and that meant Ben would be ready to go in a matter of minutes.

Her stomach lurched with a stampede of butterflies at the realization that she'd be facing all those people imminently. People who'd been there four years ago.

It seemed like only seconds until Ben stepped out of the bathroom, showered and shaved and looking far too handsome for her own good. He was adjusting a cuff link as he walked toward her, but he froze when he glanced up.

"Wow." Ben dropped his hand to his side. "Just… wow."

Chloe gazed down at herself, self-conscious and pleased at Ben's assessment. "You think?"

"You look incredible. Like a warrior princess. The belle of the battlefield."

Ben had no idea just how apt his description was, because she'd expected this event to be akin to warfare. In fact, it was part of the reason she'd chosen the shimmering gray dress.

Strapless and knee-length, she'd loved that the bodice's seams had vaguely reminded her of armor. The dress was edgy enough to make her feel like herself, but elegant enough that her mother shouldn't have too much to say about it. And then there were the shoes—strappy, studded gladiator stilettos.

"You look ready to kick ass and take names," he said. "Or at least drink lots and avoid the chicken dance."

Chloe smiled. "You're pretty wow yourself." And he was. His classic black suit, pristine white shirt and skinny black tie were classy and sophisticated. And the jacket fit his broad shoulders to perfection.

She stepped closer to his big body, walked her fingers up the placket of his shirt and under his tie. "But not quite as wow as last night," she confessed, teasing a button out of its hole. "Maybe we should stay here and I can strip you down to your most spectacular."

Ben stopped the progress of her questing fingers, grabbing her hands in his. "Nice try, coward. We've got nuptials to witness and dancing to evade."

Chloe leaned closer, raising her lips to his ear, hoping she could make his resolve wane with proximity. "What if I leave the shoes on?"

The groan that tore from his throat was wickedly sexy, and he ducked his head to capture her lips in a scorching kiss. His body was totally on board with her naughty plans, too. Chloe pressed her hips into his, encouraging him to take what he wanted. Instead, he swore and stepped back from her.

Even through her disappointment, she kind of respected him for it.

"All right," she conceded, linking her arm through his. "Let's get this over with."

Ben nodded his approval. "That's the spirit."

But as they ascended in the elevator, she could feel her bravado slipping away with every new number that lit up on their way to the twenty-fifth floor. Her grip on Ben's arm tightened when the door dinged open, and he gave her an odd look as he tugged her out into the hallway. Her trepidation grew with every formally dressed person they came upon. She kept her gaze forward to avoid making unintentional eye contact with anyone she knew.

Then they rounded the last corner, and Chloe came face-to-face with an ornate gold easel holding a placard that assured her that her time had run out.

Welcome to the Masterson–Van Allen Ceremony.

She looked up at the handsome man standing beside her who was clueless to her crimes. "There's something I should tell you."

"There's lipstick on my face, isn't there? I knew I shouldn't have kissed you, but that dress… And those goddamn shoes." He started wiping his mouth and she batted his hand away.

"There's no lipstick on you." She took a deep breath, gathering her courage. "Ben," she said, and his eyes grew serious at her use of his first name. "I haven't been to a wedding in four years."

His brow smoothed at the confession, and that damned crooked smirk he gave made it harder to breathe. "It's not like heart surgery, Chloe. Attending a wedding doesn't actually require any training. Amateurs and professionals can co-mingle freely."

Funny he should mention heart surgery, because right now her heart felt like someone had jabbed a couple of scalpels in it—lacerated and raw.

"That's not what I meant." She stared into his amber-colored eyes, searching for the calming influence he usually had on her. "What I'm trying to say is, that wedding I was at? Four years ago?"

*Just say it.*

"It was mine."

# 6

"YOU'RE MARRIED?"

He looked like she'd punched him in the solar plexus.
She supposed she sort of had.

Chloe shook her head. "I bolted."

"Sorry?"

"I ran. He said 'I do.' I said 'I can't' and took off back
down the aisle."

"Okay. Well, that's pretty big. So you're dealing with
something pretty big right now."

"Oh, it gets bigger," she assured him. "He's in there."

"What?"

"Patrick. My ex. He's in there."

"Are you serious? Why?"

"He's the son of my dad's law partner. Our families
are inextricably linked by binding contracts, forever and
ever amen."

"Why would he—"

"Come? Because etiquette dictates he should. The
same reason he was invited in the first place."

Ben shook his head. "I'm not sure what to say."

"You don't have to say anything. I just thought you
should know that you're about to walk into this room

with a pariah. People will stare and they will talk. And as my 'boyfriend,' you might not get out of this night unscathed."

"You're worried about *me*? Chloe, if ever there was a moment to think about yourself, this is it."

She hadn't even realized she was chewing at her thumbnail until Ben reached up and took her hand.

"Now c'mon. Let's get this party started, Masterson."

His support in this moment meant more than he realized. She tightened her grip on his hand, allowing herself to pretend, just for tonight, that Ben was actually more than a two-night-stand.

They were barely through the door when the onslaught began.

"Hey, Chloe!"

"Oh, hi. I didn't know you were an usher." She exchanged air kisses with the stocky, redheaded son of her father's sister.

"Yep. I clean up pretty good, huh?"

"Ben, this is my cousin Keith. Keith, this is Ben. My boyfriend," she added as an afterthought.

"Well, I knew he wasn't your husband!" Keith laughed uproariously at his own joke.

But it was only the first salvo, a preview of what she'd have to endure all evening. Even though she'd been expecting it, it stung. The reassuring warmth of Ben's hand reminded her she didn't have to weather it alone. She managed a wan smile at her prick of a cousin.

"Come on, you two. Bride's family is in the first row." He looked up at Ben, then down at their clasped hands. "You're gonna wanna hold on tight the closer we get to the front, isn't that right, Chloe?"

Chloe was relieved to find that the second shot didn't

hurt as much. They followed Keith past a human-size
vase of flowers and into the gorgeous, glass-walled room
that would house her sister's evening ceremony, with the
city of Buffalo all lit up and blanketed in snow as a back-
drop.

Everything was beautiful. Her mother would have
made sure of that. From the shimmering blue ribbons on
the chairs to the string quartet playing Pachelbel, Fiona
Masterson's style was stamped all over this wedding.
Unfortunately, Chloe couldn't appreciate the details, because from the moment they'd stepped foot in the aisle,
the bride's side of the room had erupted in whispers and
covert glances, like a tsunami of gossip moving toward
the front of the room.

Chloe's steps stuttered.

She shouldn't have come.

This was a huge mistake.

Ben gave her fingers a reassuring squeeze—which
was incredibly sweet considering her skin had gone from
zero to sweaty in two seconds flat.

Then he let go of her hand.

Her heart banged painfully against her ribs and her
scalp prickled with sweat. The whispers around her
swelled into a deafening roar. Startled at the betrayal,
Chloe's glance shot to his.

He winked at her and put his hands in his pockets.

And that small act of faith that she wasn't going to run
again, that she was strong enough to face the viper pit on
her own, steeled her resolve. The roiling nausea that had
overtaken her stomach calmed to a simmer.

Ben was right. She wasn't the coddled twenty-year-old
girl who'd been drowning in luxury and despair anymore.
She was a twenty-six-year-old woman who was making

it in the world on her own terms. Just as she'd always wanted. So she pulled her shoulders back and kept walking forward. On her own.

Ben slid into the seat beside her once they reached the front row. "That was intense. You did great, though."

"Thanks to you."

"Nah, you did all the hard stuff," he assured her, glancing around the room. "So that's the rift?" he asked. "The reason you don't get along with your parents? Because you didn't marry some Ivy Leaguer?"

Chloe glanced behind her at the reference to Patrick. She hadn't noticed him during her long walk of shame. Of course, she hadn't noticed much. It was all kind of a blur. If she wasn't sitting at the front of the room with sweaty armpits right now, she might not actually believe she'd done it.

"That's the reason I don't get along with my mother. That and the tattoos," she added. "I don't get along with my father because I dropped out of law school."

"What?" Ben's cry of disbelief came out far too loudly for her peace of mind, and she felt all the attention in the room shift back in their direction. "Sorry," he said, lowering his voice. "But what? You were going to be a lawyer?"

"According to my father I was."

The music in the room grew louder, signifying things were about to get underway, and people's eyes shifted toward the rear of the room where the mother of the bride was reveling in her walk down the aisle.

"Anything else I should know about you?" Ben whispered. "Have you ever killed a man just to watch him die?"

"Not yet. But if you talk during the ceremony and get me in trouble with the mother of the bride, I'd suggest you sleep with one eye open tonight."

THE CEREMONY WAS BEAUTIFUL, even Chloe had to admit it.

Her sister was radiant—not because of the makeup, although it looked great, even from a few feet away—but because she had a kind of deep-down radiance that made Chloe believe that she and Dalton had found true love.

After the wedding, she and Ben took the elevator up to the penthouse atrium. Unfortunately, as the sister of the bride, Chloe was expected to be in a couple of family wedding photos.

They'd barely stepped in the room before her mother pounced. "Chloe, there you are! "

"Mom." Formal air kisses. "Dad, hi." She hadn't seen him in four years, but from what she could tell, not much had changed. He still wouldn't look her in the eye. Ever since the awful evening when she'd sat beside him at the dinner table and told him that she would not be returning to law school, he'd developed a habit of looking everywhere but at her.

"Chloe." Her name sounded stiff on his lips. "Good of you to come."

She tamped down her disappointment as she and her father exchanged an awkward embrace.

He'd probably said the exact thing to every single person he'd greeted tonight. He didn't even have the courtesy to make it sound sarcastic because of her late arrival in Buffalo—at least *that* would have personalized it a little. Then again, he probably didn't even know she'd arrived late.

Desperate to keep the festivities light, her mother lunged into the fray. "Benjamin! How lovely to see you again."

"Thank you, Fiona. The pleasure is all mine. You look lovely. And what a beautiful wedding. Chloe tells me you had a hand in the decorations."

He was smooth, she'd give Ben that. Judging by her pleased preening, he'd just nailed second contact with the alien being that was her mother.

"Let me introduce you to my husband, Daryl Masterson. Senior partner with the law firm of Masterson, Grosvenor and McQuaid."

"Ben Masterson, sir. It's a pleasure to meet you."

"Masterson, is it?" her father asked, shaking Ben's hand.

"Really? No one mentioned that earlier." Chloe winced at the look her mom shot her before she turned back to Ben. "Where are you from?"

"Born and raised in Seattle, ma'am. Fiona," he corrected, and she smiled.

"I don't believe we know any Mastersons from Seattle. Daryl, do we know any Mastersons from Seattle?"

"None are coming to mind."

Ben smiled easily. "I'm sure you wouldn't be acquainted with my grandparents. And my father was adopted."

"How interesting. Isn't that interesting, Daryl? And what is it you do for a living?"

"Advertising. I'm with Carson and McLeod."

Her father nodded in approval. "Good firm, good firm. And what is it you do there?"

"Dad, seriously. Ben didn't come here for a job interview."

"I'm just checking that he's employed."

Ben placed a reassuring hand on her shoulder. She couldn't help but be impressed at how gracefully he was dealing with the inquisition. "Actually sir, I'm being considered for account director."

"A man who picks a career and follows through. I like it. Chloe could use more of that in her life."

Chloe did her best not to roll her eyes.

The buzz of his cell phone stole Daryl Masterson's attention, and he pulled it out of his breast pocket to glance at the caller ID. "Excuse me, I have to take this." He threw a, "Nice meeting you, Tim," over his shoulder as he stepped away from them.

"Don't go too far, Daryl. This won't take long and the photographer will be ready for us any minute!"

In reality, it was another half hour before the photographer was ready for them, and another hour after that before her mother finally dismissed Chloe from family wedding-picture hell. She grabbed Ben by the elbow and hauled him into the waiting elevator.

"Let's get out of here before she changes her mind!"

He hit the button for the lobby, and Chloe was relieved to be speeding away from her mother, toward the food. "Thanks for being so patient. I didn't think there were that many photo combinations for a family of four."

"And you were smiling in almost all of them. So good job."

"Hey, I can fake it with the best of them."

"You'll never have to fake it with me," he said.

Chloe shot him a sideways glance. "Are we still talking about taking pictures?"

"Oh, I'm very open to the idea of taking pictures," Ben assured her. Chloe was laughing as he grabbed her hand and they strode out of the elevator and toward the ballroom.

The room was a profusion of white flowers and fake icicles and baby-blue satin. Chloe supposed it looked like a magazine spread, but it was *waaay* too much for her. She might have a dramatic flair and heavy hand with the eye makeup, but if she ever got married, she was going to steer clear of spectacle.

"Wow. This is…a lot," Ben said beside her as they walked under a bower of flowers.

"I'm just thinking of it as a magical land I have to walk through to get to the food."

However Ben planned to respond, he was waylaid by the sudden appearance of a generously proportioned woman wearing a poufy yellow dress that made her look like Bo Peep's jaundiced grandmother.

"Chloe, darling! You're as lovely as your sister. I haven't seen you since…" Her aunt trailed off as she realized exactly when they'd last seen each other. Four years ago on a night that hadn't ended as happily as this one.

"Since my wedding day, Aunt Eileen." The reminder still stung, but Chloe felt much more equipped to deal with the inevitable stares and whispers now that she'd conquered that solo walk down the aisle.

"I… I didn't think you'd come."

"I knew you'd come," interjected Eileen's husband as he trundled up to them. "I just didn't think you'd stay 'til the end!" The portly man punctuated the joke with a wheezing guffaw.

"Hilarious, Uncle Phil." Chloe leaned forward for the obligatory cheek kiss. "If you two will excuse us, I see people eating bacon-wrapped shrimp and I want to be one of them." She grabbed Ben's hand and tugged him farther into the ballroom, doing her best to avoid more prying relatives as they approached a white-suited waiter carrying a silver tray laden with champagne flutes.

"You do want a drink, right?" she asked, dropping his hand and snagging two glasses of bubbly. He accepted the one she held in his direction.

"I probably just lost one of the most lucrative contracts my agency's ever bid on, and this is an open bar. You're damn right I'm having a drink."

Chloe stopped with her glass halfway to her lips. "Oh, my God! Ben! I'm such an ass! I was so caught up in my own drama I didn't even ask how your meeting went."

"It was less than stellar," he said, running a hand through his hair. "Burke was not buying into the Masterson charm. He's old-school and he doesn't seem to have much respect for Carson and McLeod. And he thinks I'm a child playing at a man's job."

Chloe was outraged. "He said that?"

"Not in so many words, but I'm fluent in subtext."

"Do you want to talk about it?" she asked.

"Nope." Ben clinked his glass against hers before he brought the champagne to his lips and took an impressively long gulp.

Chloe mirrored his actions. Liquid courage always helped when she was dealing with her family and the looming threat of running into Patrick. She took another fortifying sip before she and Ben headed out in search of the bacon-wrapped shrimp.

When they arrived at table one, as per the seating chart, her parents were already there. Her father, much to no one's surprise, was on his phone again.

"There you two are!" Her mother gave her a stern look when she saw Chloe's fist-full of shrimp skewers.

"Take a seat! I wanted to finish the conversation we started before the wedding photos. How old did you say you were again, Benjamin?"

Ben held out Chloe's chair before taking his seat beside Fiona.

"Thirty, ma'am."

"Thirty. That's very young to be up for such a big promotion. Chloe's twenty-six and has yet to settle on a career path. It's nice to see her with someone who's so focused."

Chloe's mother flashed him a beaming smile that was usually reserved for the benefactors of her charities—and for sharks circling bleeding disaster victims treading water miles from shore. Chloe could feel a tiny drop of fear trickling along the back of her neck, heading for her spine.

Fiona Masterson was about to try and talk Ben into making a down payment on her eldest daughter. Upgrading from boyfriend to fiancé.

Chloe could not have been more relieved when the emcee just then took the stage to announce the arrival of the happy couple.

Amidst the applause and catcalls as Mr. and Mrs. Van Allen made their way toward the head table, Ben slung his arm across the back of her chair and leaned toward her. His breath was warm on her ear and, combined with the champagne bubbling in her empty stomach, made her feel a bit woozy in the best possible way.

"I have no idea what your problem is with your parents. They seem nice."

Chloe laughed at the devilish glint in his eye. He was teasing her. "Of course they seem nice to you! They love you!"

Ben's modest grin let her know she'd reacted appropriately to his bait. "Well, I do give good parent."

"You sure do. My mom was practically swooning and my dad stayed off his phone for almost four minutes. That's a new record, *Tim*. Which reminds me…not to brag or anything, but I totally nailed you."

Ben cocked an eyebrow. "Yeah, you did. And I liked it, so if you want to do it again later, I'm in."

"Gross! No!" She punched him in the arm. "I meant I nailed *your job*. I guessed right on the plane. You're in advertising."

"Guilty as charged."

"*Ugh*. No law references around my parents, please."

Ben leaned forward and pressed a quick kiss to her lips.

She tried not to blush. "What was that for?"

He shrugged. "Because you're doing great. And because I get it."

"Get what?"

"I get why you didn't want to come here. I think a hundred people have made the same joke at your expense by now. But they don't understand that what you did took guts. The thought of quitting my job makes me nauseous, even though I occasionally feel like it's stifling me. Like it's not what I'm supposed to be doing."

Chloe leaned forward and kissed him back.

"What was that for?"

"Because sometimes, Masterson, you're really good at knowing exactly what to say."

By the time they'd eaten, listened to lame wedding speeches, and witnessed every conceivable variation of fathers and brides, mothers and grooms, and bridesmaids and groomsmen sway together to sentimental pop drivel, Chloe was actually enjoying herself. Most everyone with a runaway-bride comment had delivered their joke, and people were finally focusing more on the party than on her past.

And Ben had been an amazing wingman, guiding her through the night with very little damage. Plus, he was pretty freakin' cute. And so good in bed. Like, really, really good, she decided as she watched him fend off the advances of one of her cousins on his way back from the bathroom.

"Your cousin Amber says hi." He folded himself into the chair beside her.

"Yeah, right." She glanced over to where her cousin stood, her eyes still glued to Ben. Not that Chloe blamed her. Ben had loosened his tie and popped the top button on his shirt, so he was looking pretty damn sexy right now. Chloe raised a hand to her cousin and wiggled her fingers in a wave that earned her a glare before Amber stomped off to try her luck with some other target.

"Excuse me. Can I have your attention please?" Her sister's fiancé, no, *husband*, Chloe reminded herself, had grabbed the DJ's mic and a hush settled over the crowd. "Hey, everyone! Are you guys enjoying the party?"

Applause and catcalls answered the question.

"Before we hand this dance over to DJ Spinnicus," more applause and catcalls from the younger attendees, "I wanted to take a second to tell my beautiful bride how much I love her, and how glad I am that our lovely mothers, who sit on the Children's Hospital board together, set us up on that blind date, because I can't imagine my life without her."

Cue the obligatory romantic "awwwww" from the crowd.

"And I also want to wish her a very happy birthday! So to honor what has become a bit of a Masterson family tradition—"

"Oh no." Chloe shook her head.

"—I thought you might all help me serenade the birthday girl on her wedding day. You know the words!"

"Nuh-uh. This can't be happening."

"What? What's happening?" Ben asked.

A familiar riff filled the ballroom, and the wedding guests went crazy as the screen behind Dalton lit up with a slideshow of the happy couple, and everyone began singing along.

"No way!" Ben exclaimed, but she was already laughing at herself, at the situation, at the expression of incredulity on Ben's face. "Is *this* why you hate the song?" He laughed, shaking his head. "You're jealous of your sister? Pathetic, Masterson. I expected better of you."

"You were never, ever supposed to know about this," she gasped through her giggles. Her crying sister ran up onstage to kiss Dalton, who was manfully belting his way through the lyrics with no attention to whether he was in tune. Chloe would never admit it aloud, but it was all kind of sweet and romantic.

Ben drained his beer, and placed the bottle on the table with a *thunk* that she could hear even over the sing-a-long.

"Come on," he said, standing and holding out his hand to her.

"Are we leaving?" she asked, wiping her eyes, hoping that her tears of laughter hadn't tracked mascara down her cheeks. She grabbed his hand and he yanked her to her feet.

"Oh, hell no! We're going to dance, Masterson." She yelped as Ben twirled her, startling another peal of laughter from her before he tugged her onto the dance floor.

"You need to get over yourself and respect the man, nay, the *legend*, that is Neil Diamond," he lectured, pulling her into his arms just in time to sing-shout "ba ba baaa" before spinning her away again.

By the time the song was over, not only had Chloe joined in for a couple of "ba ba baaas" and some "so goods," but she had a new appreciation for Caroline—both the song and her sister. Neil Diamond, she decided, wasn't half bad. And neither was Ben.

He leaned in but he still had to yell over the applause. "You want some water?"

"Yes, please!"

"I'll meet you back at the table," he said, heading through the throng of dancing guests toward the closest bar.

Chloe headed in the opposite direction, wiping her brow. She was having fun, she realized as she flopped into her chair.

"I thought you hated this song."

The familiar voice was a punch in the gut, and her good mood soured a little. "Patrick."

He plunked himself down in the chair beside her, Ben's chair, and took a gulp of his beer.

"I see you brought a date."

"Didn't you?"

"It didn't seem appropriate."

She flinched at the censure in his words and the alcohol on his breath. "It's been four years."

"So? You think people have forgotten?"

Chloe shook her head. "No. I'm *sure* people haven't forgotten. But they've moved on, for the most part. I guess I'd just hoped that maybe you'd forgiven me by now."

"Forgiven you? For embarrassing me in front of my entire social circle? And now you're here, dancing, making a spectacle of yourself. Do you understand how this looks to people?"

"I haven't done anything wrong. We were twenty-two years old. Kids. We had no business getting married. We weren't in love. You were just trying to get in good with my father. And so was I. I'm sorry that I hurt you, just like I'm sorry if you're embarrassed to be here. But if it's that bad, then maybe you shouldn't have come."

"Shouldn't have come? You know that wasn't an option."

Chloe nodded. "Yeah, I know."

She was sad for Patrick. He wasn't the quick-to-smile kid she remembered. And she felt bad for her part in that, but she'd made the right decision, and she refused to regret it, despite the fallout.

Chloe reached for her wine, more for something to occupy her hands than because she really wanted any. Still, she was shocked when Patrick snatched the glass from her hand. "You've had enough."

Chloe's brain had barely reacted to the douchebag move when a bottle of water appeared on the table in front of her.

"Is there a problem here?"

"Yes." Patrick stood and drew up to his full height. Ben still had four inches on him. "The problem is that my ex-fiancée is singing and dancing and making a fool of herself. People are starting to talk."

"Well, I think you might be mistaken. From where I'm standing, it looks like my *girlfriend* is celebrating her sister's big day, having a really good time without you, and people have been talking the entire night. If that's a problem for you, feel free to leave."

Patrick opened his mouth to say more, but even in his slightly inebriated state, his common sense kicked in. With a mumbled, "Whatever," he slunk away, disappearing into the crowd.

A tingly sensation spread through Chloe's body, like she had carbonation in her blood.

"What? Why are you looking at me like that?" Ben asked, amber eyes wary.

"You fought for me. That's pretty cool."

Ben scoffed. "I didn't fight for you. I had a conversation with a total dick for you."

"Still pretty cool."

Ben's chuckle made her feel warm and throbby. "You want to get out of here?"

Chloe took a swig from the water bottle. "More than anything."

THE TRIP UP to their room was a magical blur of stolen kisses and sweet relief. Chloe had survived her sister's wedding, and she was in the mood to celebrate.

"You're really sexy when you're defending my honor, you know that, Ben Masterson of the Seattle Mastersons?"

She wound her arms around his neck, kissing his ear, his cheek, his neck, whatever she could reach, loving the pressure of his steadying arm around her waist.

Ben unlocked the door and pulled her inside. "I'm really sexy all the time," he told her, stepping so close that she had to look up to see his eyes, even in her kick-ass shoes.

He cradled her face with his hands and Chloe's breath shook as she exhaled. Heat rolled from his body, bewitching her senses. The feel of him, the sounds, the scent. No cologne, just warm skin. Simple. Manly. Intoxicating.

His thumbs brushed her cheeks, his fingers slid into her hair, and he lowered his head. The sweet thrill of his lips against hers paralyzed her. Ben's kisses always seemed to knock the wind from her, make her gasp. She was helpless to move as her world narrowed to just their mingling breaths and the sweet pressure of his mouth as he started walking her farther into the room.

Then he spun her around and pressed her up against the wall. The paint was cool against her skin, and Ben was hard and warm as he molded himself to her back. The dichotomy was hot as hell. Especially when he started kissing her neck…

"Oh, God. Ben," she breathed as his right hand grazed her breast, caressing it, setting her on fire. His hand continued its sensual journey down the front of her body, and she resented the dress she'd loved hours earlier, as it blocked her aching skin from the hand skimming over her stomach, her thigh, lower. Finally his warm palm reached her knee, and when he began the journey back up her leg, he slipped his hand underneath her dress. Now there was nothing but the erotic heat of skin against skin as his fingers tracked up to her inner thigh. It felt incredible, his hands on her like this. Chloe braced her palms against the wall, opening her legs, pushing her ass against his erection.

He groaned as he dug his fingers inside her panties, and she thought she might pass out from the pleasure.

"You're so wet."

She could only sigh in response as his finger invaded her.

BEN PLUNGED ANOTHER finger into her slick wetness, and her whimper of pleasure went straight to his groin. She started chanting his name, low and pleading, and he was sure he'd never experienced anything as erotic as this moment.

"I'm so close," she whispered.

He could feel her on the precipice, wanted so badly to give her what she craved.

Ben dropped his other hand to her clit, rubbing her through the damp lace even as he sped the rhythm of his fingers inside her. Her knees buckled as she came and she gave a sweet cry of release.

She was panting as she turned in his arms, her hair disheveled, her breasts on the verge of escaping her dress. Her satisfied smile was so goddamned sexy.

"Come to bed with me." He barely recognized his own voice, the words were rough.

Chloe's grin was naughty. "I'm not sure I can walk," she teased.

"I can work with that," he said, scooping her over his shoulder in the fireman's hold. Chloe's scream of surprise became laughter as he hauled her toward the bed and gave her a slap on the ass before dropping her on the giant mattress.

He shucked his suit jacket and crawled onto the bed, but when he tried to take charge, Chloe wasn't having any of it.

"Uh-uh." She shook her head, a hand on his chest. "It's my turn to explore," she told him. And that was how he found himself flat on his back, staring up at a sexy vision as she reached for the zipper that ran down the side of her body. The sparkly gray dress began to gape as his temptress lowered the zipper inch by seductive inch.

Finally, the fabric fell open to reveal a strapless red lace push-up bra and a whole bunch of warm, willing Chloe.

Ben groaned as she pushed the dress down over her hips—the red lace panties were as sexy to look at as they'd been to touch—and finally the dress was gone and she was reaching for the buckle of one strappy studded high-heel.

"You said you'd leave the shoes on." Ben wasn't sure if it was an order or he was begging.

Chloe frowned playfully. "Hey, I thought I was in charge here."

"You leave those shoes on and I'll do anything you want." *Begging. Definitely begging.*

Her smile signified the complete shift in power. "Well, how can I refuse an offer like that?" She crawled toward him, and her breasts looked so amazingly soft and perfect. Then she was straddling his hips and tugging off his tie and unbuttoning his shirt, and he was lost.

She dropped kisses along his chest as she bared it, then his stomach. He tore his shirt the rest of the way off as she fumbled with his belt buckle, and he loved the look of concentration on her face. She was amazing. Sweet and edgy and sexy and real, all wrapped up in a cute little package that drove him wild. Then his belt came undone and he stopped thinking altogether.

She divested him of his shoes, his socks and finally his Calvin Kleins. Then she ran her hands up his thighs, and his breath stuttered with the pleasure. His hips flexed involuntarily as she drew ever nearer to the part of him that wanted her most. Ben didn't know what he was expecting from that moment, but the sudden wet heat as she dragged her tongue the length of his shaft ripped a groan from his chest and he swore at the overwhelming sensation.

When she slipped him into her mouth, her fingers squeezing the base of his cock, the warm suction made his hips jerk.

"God. Chloe. I want to be inside you so bad."

He reached down and dragged her up his body, kissing her as he rolled her onto her back. He paused to drink in the sight of her lying there in sexy red lingerie and do-me heels, wanting him. Thankfully he'd left his suitcase beside the bed, because he was half-mad with lust for her, and he wasn't going to be able to hold out much longer.

He had the condom on in record time, looking up from

his task as Chloe popped the front clasp on her bra. Her breasts were beautiful, and he ached to feel them pressed against his chest as he took her.

He dragged her panties down her thighs, and she raised her knees so he could pull them past her shoes. And then there was nothing separating them. Ben positioned himself between her legs, staring into her eyes as he slid home into the slick, smooth heat of her.

His name was a gasp on her lips as they moved together, and Ben tried to take it slow, but her nails were digging into his back and she was meeting him thrust for thrust, and things got out of control before he knew it. She wrapped her leg around his hip a split second before she came apart in his arms, and the aftershocks of her orgasm started his own. He gave in to the sharp wave of ecstasy and let himself drown in it.

MORNING CAME TOO EARLY, as it always did, in Chloe's opinion. Despite the early hour, Chloe found herself smiling as she indulged in a sleepy stretch. The reason for her good mood was slung out on his stomach, his arm nestled against the underside of her breasts, his stubbly chin resting on her shoulder and his lips close to her neck.

"What was that?"

"What was what?" he mumbled into her hair.

"The whole macho caveman thing? Carrying me off to bed and having your way with me? That was kinda hot, Masterson. I didn't think you had it in you."

"Yeah, right. Everything about me screams sex god. You knew what you were getting into."

Chloe laughed as he pulled her closer, kissing her neck before levering his big body out of bed. Chloe enjoyed the view, especially when he turned and began rooting through his suitcase. Ben Masterson was in possession of one very fine ass.

She pushed up on one elbow, clutching the sheet to her breasts with her other hand. "Where are you going?" she asked with an overly dramatic moue.

"Shower. Why, you wanna join me?"

"Forget it." Chloe flopped back into the lavish bed, stretching luxuriously. "I am on vacation, sort of, and when I'm on vacation, I don't go anywhere until the glowing red numbers on that devil machine over there start with at *least* an eight." She made a halfhearted gesture in the general vicinity of the alarm clock.

"C'mon, Chloe. Get up. Greet the day. You know what they say about early birds."

"Whatever, drone. Tell the Man I said hi." She snuggled deeper into the pillows.

"Fine," he relented, closing his suitcase. He faced her, slinging his jeans and a white T-shirt over his shoulder. "You've got twenty minutes of peace while I shower and shave. But in return, you have to order room service."

"Deal." Chloe lifted a hand. "Pass me the menu?"

"Are you kidding me?" He reached behind him to grab the leather-bound menu from the ornate desk, lobbing it so it landed squarely on her stomach with a soft *thwump*. "Such a diva."

"Not my fault." Chloe picked up the menu and leafed through the gold-lettered pages. "Let's put the blame on this king-size bed, where it belongs."

Ben shook his head. "This bed is turning out to be more trouble than I expected."

"The good stuff always is. No worms on the menu, Mr. Early Bird. You might have to settle for waffles."

"Mmm. Syrupy." He leaned over and pressed a kiss to her lips. As startled as Chloe was by the familiarity, she was even more startled that she didn't mind. He was not what she'd expected from the corporate poster boy who'd struck up a conversation on the plane. She couldn't help her grin as she watched him and his cute butt pad toward the bathroom wearing nothing but a pair of tube socks.

The shower flipped on, and Chloe reclined on the mountain of pillows behind her, abandoning her menu-perusal duties now that Ben was gone. Instead, she nestled into the plush bedding and mentally relived some of last night's more memorable moments.

By the time the water flipped off, she found that her dirty mind was sort of regretting turning down Ben's offer for a tandem shower. She'd begun to formulate a plan to entice him into a second one when a knock at the door startled her back to reality.

"Who the hell?" she wondered with a glance at the clock. It seemed someone else was breaking her pre-eight in the morning rule.

Chloe was in the midst of wrapping a sheet around herself when the insistent knock sounded again. "Coming!" she called, but she was trapped on the bed for a moment until she located her abandoned stilettos. Shoving her feet into them, she hurried to the door as quickly as the unbuckled death traps would allow. "Coming," she called again.

She wrenched the door open, shocked to find a distinguished man in a suit with a full head of white hair and a bushy white mustache. He looked equally surprised to see her standing there in nothing but a bunched-up sheet and last night's heels.

Clearing his throat, he glanced at the girl beside him in the hallway. She was tall and thin, probably about fourteen, and her attention didn't waver from her iPhone for even a second.

"I'm terribly sorry to disturb you, miss. I thought this was Ben Masterson's room," the gentleman said, making a move to leave, but as though his name had conjured the man, Ben pulled open the door to the bathroom, a white towel slung around his hips, and another draped around his shoulders as he rubbed one end over his wet hair.

"Is room service here already?" he asked, then froze as he spotted the man. Chloe noticed the kid had finally looked up from her phone. Not that she blamed her. Ben's bare chest was a pretty powerful draw.

"Mr. Burke!"

*Uh-oh.* This was the hotel guy? The head honcho? Chloe realized, in retrospect, that smeared makeup, a bed sheet and stilettos might not have been the most inspired fashion choice for this moment.

"Mr. Masterson." The address dripped with censure.

Chloe knew Ben was panicked because he stepped right out onto the carpet with bare feet, cellulitis be damned.

"Sir, I apologize for the towel. I wasn't expecting you. I'd like you to meet Chloe...my wife."

# 7

"HAVE YOU LOST your mind?"

He'd expected the rage. Hell, he probably deserved it. He was just thankful she'd held it in check until their surprise visitors had headed off toward the dining room to procure a table for the breakfast meeting he and Chloe were about to attend with them.

"Don't you get it? It's a test, Chloe. That means I'm still in the running. He told me we were having lunch, but he showed up for breakfast—with his granddaughter. He wants to know if I can handle myself, and, by extension, his business when the shit hits the fan. This is my chance for redemption. Did you see the look on his face when I walked out of the bathroom? I couldn't tell him I'd spent the night with a woman I met on the plane!"

"This is a horrible idea, Ben."

"But you'll do it?"

There was a long, heart-stopping pause as he watched a dozen expressions fight for dominance in her stunning eyes.

Her huff let him know he'd won.

"Fine. I'll go to this stupid breakfast with you."

Relief flooded through him in waves.

"You'll pretend to be married to me?"

She rolled her eyes. "Yes. You suffered through an entire wedding with me. It's only fair."

"You're the best, Chloe. Seriously." He hurried over to the bed, searching for the suit pants he'd worn to the wedding. Ben grabbed them off the floor and reached into the left pocket, fumbling with his wallet for a moment before holding his hand in her direction. "Here. Put this on."

"What? What the—? Is this a ring? Did you just pull *a ring* out of your wallet? Did you have that with you the whole time?"

Ben winced at his blunder. Guess he should have laid a little groundwork before springing the ring on her, but he was in kind of a hurry. "Just put it on, okay?"

"You said you were single! Single and, quote *'loving it'* end quote. Why the hell do you have a ring with you?"

"Relax. I am single. I swear. It's not what you're thinking. I just carry it around as a reminder," he added. Leaving out the "to never be so stupid as to end up married because women are nothing but trouble," because he liked irony better when it wasn't happening to him.

"What, it's a good luck charm or something?"

"Or something," Ben said.

Chloe looked skeptical. "It's still weird," she said, but to his infinite relief she slid the ring onto the appropriate finger, holding it up for inspection.

He wondered what she thought of it—a modest diamond flanked by two deep purple amethysts. A simple ring. Elegant, he'd always believed, though Mel had disagreed when he'd gotten down on one knee to give it to her. She'd been more into the idea of something "newer" with a "bigger diamond."

"This is really pretty," she said after a moment. "I

love amethysts. They make everything look so elegant," Chloe said, and his head snapped toward her.

"I'm still weirded out by the fact that you keep a ring in your wallet, though," she grumbled. "That's creepy. I'm talking serial-killer creepy. Putting this on had better not have made me the Bride of Death or something equally messed up," she warned. "I don't want to find out that all the ring's previous owners are dead and I'm next."

Ben smiled in spite of himself. "Well, you're not totally off the mark. It was my grandma's wedding ring. She left it to me when she died. Natural causes," he assured her, and the joke defused some tension.

He walked over to the armoire and pulled out two of his suits—the gray one from the plane and a navy one— holding them up for Chloe's inspection. "Which of these will best erase the memory of seeing me in a towel and re-establish me as a competent professional?" he asked.

"The navy one is extremely boring. I'd go with that," Chloe advised, rooting through her suitcase. "I'm just going to wear jeans, a T-shirt and a black blazer, because I'm pretty sure I didn't pack anything that says 'sorry we met while I was dressed like a slut.'"

"Don't worry about it," Ben said. "You never have to apologize to a man for that."

"BEN, SO GLAD you and your lovely wife could join us." The distinguished elderly man rose to his feet, and exchanged a swift shake with Ben before extending his hand to Chloe as well. "Chloe, thank you for coming. Please accept my apologies for our unorthodox meeting this morning. I wasn't aware Ben was traveling with such a lovely companion. He didn't mention he was married in our meeting."

"Consider it forgotten. My husband is all business on

these trips. Sometimes I think he forgets I'm even along for the ride. So thank you for inviting me, Mr. Burke. This is a lovely hotel you have."

"Why, thank you, my dear. And please, call me Edward."

Chloe nodded and sat in the chair Ben held out for her. She was disgusted with herself at how easily she could still fall back into the niceties of polite society. Fiona Masterson had trained her well.

Edward gestured to the young girl. "This is my granddaughter, Kenley."

The sullen teen glanced up from her phone in momentary acknowledgment, but her thumbs never stilled on the screen. She was wearing a plaid, flannel shirt unbuttoned over a My Little Pony T-shirt and thick-rimmed glasses that were probably fake, and Chloe would have bet a substantial amount there were some Doc Martens hidden under the table, if anyone were offering odds on it.

"Kenley, what did we discuss?"

With a put-upon sigh, Kenley set her phone facedown on the table beside her. Edward gave a "kids these days" shrug of apology before calling the waitress over to take their breakfast orders. Once that was taken care of, he and Ben got down to business.

Chloe sipped gingerly at her coffee as she waited for her waffles to arrive.

"This is boring."

Hearing Kenley speak in actual words startled her— she'd grown so used to the girl's sighs and theatrical movement of limbs—but Chloe couldn't argue with her assessment of reach and revenue and target markets.

"I like your makeup."

Oh, man. Were they having a conversation now? "Thanks," Chloe replied, hoping monosyllables might be her ticket out of whatever weird thing was happening on this side of the table.

*Just pick up your phone,* she willed the little hipster. *Gramps isn't paying attention anymore. Ben's wowing him with jargon. Take advantage.*

"How do you do that? That wingy eyeliner thing? It looks good."

*Definitely* a conversation. But at least now an interesting one.

"It's easy," she said, earning a withering look. Teen wrath at its finest, Chloe had a moment of empathy for the girl's parents. "A little bit of practice, and you'll be an expert in no time."

"Oh." The tiny spark of life that had been there a minute ago extinguished, and just like that, she was back to being a Mopey McMoperson.

*Well, crap.* Chloe pushed her coffee aside and reached into her purse. "Here." She pulled out her makeup bag and plopped it on the table.

Kenley's eyes rounded behind the irony of her fake, plastic-rimmed glasses. "Wow."

"Kid, you ain't seen nothing yet," she assured her, spilling its contents across the tablecloth.

She smiled a bit at the awestruck look on Kenley's face, but only because Chloe was sure that it was the same look of dazed euphoria that she herself always wore while stepping over the threshold of Sephora.

"Give me your napkin," Chloe ordered. After a bit of rummaging, she managed to locate a pen in her cavernous purse, and when she looked up, it was to find Kenley holding up a white square of cloth.

Chloe shook her head. "Swanky restaurants are the worst," she lamented, shoving her hand back into her bag and producing a couple of crumpled receipts. "We'll just have to make do."

Smoothing one out the best she could, Chloe sketched a quick picture of an eye, complete with lashes and brow. Then she plucked her liquid eyeliner from the melee of makeup. "Okay, here's what you do…"


BEN NOTICED CHLOE and Kenley giggling over a pile of receipts, a dozen shades of eye shadow spread across the table before them. Neither of them had made much of a dent in their breakfasts.

"So what do you think, Mr. Masterson?"

"Huh?" Ben turned his attention back to Burke.

The man smiled. "You seem a little distracted."

*Shit.* "Yeah. No! Mr. Burke, I assure you that if you choose Carter and McLeod to represent Hotel Burke, we will work with laser-precision focus to promote your brand and—"

"Please, son. I recognize the look of a man enchanted by his lady. I'm old, but I'm not dead, and I certainly don't need you to blow smoke up my arse. I'm well aware of your agency's reputation. You wouldn't be here if I wasn't already impressed."

*Impressed? Huh.* After yesterday's meeting, Ben had been sure the firm fell somewhere below root canal on Edward Burke's list of *Things That Are Awful*.

"Thank you, sir. We at Carter and McLeod work hard to exceed expectations."

The old man leaned in. "You're here because it's important to me that I know the man behind the scene. And I have to say, you surprised me today."

*Uh-oh.* Ben could feel the deal slipping away.

"Yesterday, I'd made up my mind about you. I thought you were confident to the point of being cocky—" He held up a hand to silence Ben's defense. "Which is not necessarily a bad thing," he continued. "However, I didn't think you were a fit for my hotel. This is, at heart, a family business. And I didn't believe you truly understood that. Today, you changed my mind."

"If you'll just— I… What?"

Burke took a sip of his coffee. "You really impressed me today. Not only do you obviously know your stuff, but more importantly, you have your priorities in order."

Ben didn't mean to glance at Chloe again. It just happened.

"As you've no doubt surmised, Mr. Masterson, my showing up at your hotel room unannounced this morning was a strategic move. Anyone can be impressive with the right preparation and enough notice. It's the hiccups in life, the moments you didn't see coming, that tell me who I'm really dealing with."

Ben followed Edward Burke's gaze to the other side of the table. Kenley looked happy and engaged, nothing like the sullen, phone-addicted girl he's met earlier.

And Chloe…well, her smile was really something when she had her guard down.

"Today I got a glimpse of who you are during the hiccups. So you send the contracts over, and I'll have my legal team take a gander at the fine print. After that, Mr. Masterson, I'd say we have a deal."

Ben did his best to avoid any outward manifestations of fist-pumping, victory dances and expletive-laced exclamations, but his handshake definitely had more vigor than it had at the conclusion of yesterday's meeting.

"Thank you, sir. You've made a great choice in Carson and McLeod."

"Only by extension, Ben. You're the choice I made here. And I hope it's a great one."

"I won't let you down."

"Grandpa, I really need to use my phone, quick. Chloe has this awesome YouTube channel and I want to subscribe." Mr. Burke nodded and the phone was a blur, Kenley grabbed it so fast.

With a final round of goodbyes and more handshakes, Ben and Chloe wound their way through the restaurant, dodging tables as they walked toward the dining room's grandiose entrance.

"You look pretty pleased with yourself."

Ben nodded, jamming his hands in his pockets as he and Chloe stepped into the lobby. "That would be a fair assessment of my current state, yes."

"I take it that means the meeting went well."

"'Well' does not even begin to describe it. The meeting was great. Beyond great. It was the meeting all other meetings aspire to be. Baby meetings will grow up hearing the legendary tales of this meeting, hoping one day to be just like it."

She grinned at him. "Congratulations, Ben. I'm really happy for you."

"Thank you. I'm actually really happy for me, too. Except for the giant-wife-shaped lie I had to tell to get me to this point, everything is going according to plan. By the way, what was all that about back there?"

"What was what about?" she asked innocently, but Ben wasn't buying it, even with the raise he was going to get when Carson and McLeod promoted him to account director for landing Hotel Burke.

"Don't play coy with me. You know I'm talking about Kenley and her phone and her sudden desperate need to connect to Wi-Fi."

"It's nothing," she said as they passed the ballroom that had hosted Caroline's wedding the night before.

"Lies! You have a YouTube channel! I want to hear all about it."

"Let's change the subject," she countered, but there was no real heat to her words, and he was in far too good a mood to deny himself the pleasure of teasing her.

"If I guess will you tell me?"

"Can't you just focus on gloating about your better-than-great meeting?"

"Do you do acoustic covers of Neil Diamond songs on your channel?"

Chloe rolled her eyes.

"It's makeup, isn't it? I saw you teaching Kenley."

"Just forget it."

"No way. You were so smug about nailing my occupation, but I got yours, too!"

"What? No, you didn't."

"Sure. I said artist. You're a makeup artist. That counts."

Chloe's eyes widened. She looked a little...stunned?

"Come on! I want details."

He could see that she wanted to tell him. She didn't quite believe that he was really interested, but she definitely wanted to tell him.

"It's nothing," she averred. "I just post stuff about—"

"What are you two doing out here?"

Ben turned to find Chloe's sister, husband in tow, shooing them toward another overly decorated room.

"You're supposed to be inside already. Dalton and I are about to make our big entrance. You should be sitting down, eating these fab mini-quiches I picked for brunch, and waiting for us."

*OH, CRAP.* The gift opening. She'd completely forgotten about it after she and Ben had gotten caught in flagrante by a hotel mogul and had to pretend they were—

"Ohmygosh, Chloe! Are you engaged?"

*Double crap.* She hadn't taken off the damn ring.

Caroline had her left hand in a death grip before Chloe had finished the thought.

She glanced to Ben for support, but the coward was backing away, pointing toward the entrance to the gift opening and mouthing "I'll be by the mini-quiches," before he disappeared.

Chloe tried to pull away, but it was no use.

"Dalton, look. My sister's engaged. Why didn't you tell me, Chloe? This is so exciting! How did he ask you? When did he ask you? Ohmygosh, tell me everything!"

"Caro—"

"You should totally get married in the summer. *This* summer! Have you chosen colors yet?"

"No, we're not getting—"

"Great! I have so many ideas. You and I didn't get to plan my wedding together, but maybe we can plan yours. I mean, I'll be in Europe for the next three months, but we can Skype. Are you going to do it here, or in Seattle?"

Chloe tried to wedge a word into her sister's soliloquy, wondering what had happened to the calm, poised woman she'd hung out with yesterday afternoon. Before she could open her mouth to set her sister straight, Caroline spun Chloe around by the hand. "Ohmygosh, Mom! Chloe's engaged!"

Time stopped.

Chloe could barely breathe. Her mother was staring at her.

"You're engaged?" Fiona Masterson's voice was little more than a whisper. Her eyes were brimming with tears. She looked at Chloe. Really looked at her. Not with sadness, or disapproval, or disappointment—but with hope.

"Yep, we're engaged!" Chloe stuck out her left hand as proof.

And then the most astounding thing happened.

Her mother hugged her. *Hugged* her.

"Oh, Chloe, honey, I'm so happy for you. This is wonderful news. Just wonderful! Wait until your father hears about this!"

"Why didn't you say anything earlier?" Caroline asked.

"We just…" Chloe grappled for something that didn't sound completely asinine. "We just didn't want to steal your thunder." Caroline's beaming smile told her she'd picked the right angle, so Chloe continued. "I mean, this is your time. Your day."

"Oh, goodness! Chloe's right!" Her mom jumped back into party mode. "You two are already late. We need to get in there."

Chloe exhaled as her mother, her sister and Dalton disappeared into the conference room full of presents and decorations and people eating brunch.

*What the hell had she just done?*

Ben was, as promised, standing by the buffet. "These are actually really delicious," he said around a mouthful of mini-quiche. "I had the asparagus and bacon one, and also the dill, ham and smoked-gouda kind."

"Good to know. Maybe we can have them at our wedding."

Ben swallowed. "Ha. Yes. Definitely." He grabbed another one from the four-tiered serving platter with a pretty little place card advertising Caramelized Onion & Prosciutto Mini-Quiche. "And speaking of our nonexistent wedding, you got everything straightened out? Explained the truth? How'd they take it?"

"Huh?" Chloe realized she was twisting the ring on her left finger and quickly pulled her hands apart. If by "straightened out," he meant "let them believe what they want," then sure. And what did it matter anyway? She was catching a plane back to her real life in a few hours. She would never see Ben again. That was the whole point, wasn't it? The reason she'd fallen into bed with him in the first place. Why ruin their perfectly imperfect moment in time?

Ben didn't need to know that her family thought they were engaged. She would just call her mom once they were on opposite sides of the country again, and tell her the engagement was off, and life would get back to normal.

But at least when it did, she could hold on to the memory of what it had felt like to have her mother's approval.

"Oh, wow. Chloe, seriously. You have to taste this." Ben shoved the other half of the savory tartlet in her mouth and Chloe was grateful for the distraction.

Saved by the mini-quiche.

It *was* pretty delicious.

ONE HOUR AND Caroline's entire wedding registry later, Ben and Chloe were in their room again. Her sister was an efficient gift-opener, had to give her that.

She'd hugged Chloe tight and promised to Skype at least once a week when she returned from her honeymoon. Her dad had continued to look everywhere but at her as they said awkward goodbyes, and her mother had given her another hug instead of the usual air kisses, and even told her that she'd done a beautiful job on Caroline's wedding makeup. Chloe was still reeling from that one.

It was funny how things turned out sometimes. Forty-eight hours ago, she couldn't wait to get home to Seattle, and now...now Chloe wasn't quite in such a hurry.

"You got everything?" Ben asked, handing her the brush she'd left in the bathroom.

She threw it on top of the rest of the stuff in her suitcase. "Yeah. I think so."

"When does your flight leave?"

"In about an hour and a half. Yours?"

"Not until five tonight. Burke's second-in-command is going to give me a tour of the place at two so that I can better understand his brand." Ben wet his lips, glanced at his watch. "But I guess you should get going so you have plenty of time to get to the airport and check in and stuff."

Chloe pulled the zipper shut on her suitcase. She shrugged into her coat and grabbed her purse, but when she turned back, Ben had already scooped up her luggage.

"You okay?"

Her reply was a one-shouldered shrug. "I'm really going to miss…this bed. California King. You don't run into too many of those, you know."

"Aww. Don't get all sentimental on me, Masterson. You'll meet other beds." They shared a flickering smile. "Let me walk you downstairs?"

Chloe nodded. "As long as 'walk' means 'take the elevator.'"

The ride down was silent. No silly Neil Diamond jokes. No bickering. No making out. For the first time since they'd met—had it really only been two days ago?—neither of them seemed to know what to say or do.

When they reached the lobby, Ben caught the concierge's eye. "May I help you, sir?"

"Yes, the lady needs a taxi to the airport."

"One will be along momentarily. I'll have the doorman come and get you when it arrives." Ben nodded in thanks.

They stood there awkwardly for a moment.

"Oh!" Chloe pried the ring off her finger. "You probably want this back," she said, holding it out to him.

"Yeah. Yes. Thank you for remembering."

Electricity crackled up her arm when their fingertips brushed during the exchange. Ben tucked his grandmother's ring into his wallet.

"This is really weird." Chloe couldn't help but point out the obvious. It seemed to ease the tension a little bit. "It's like we're getting divorced or something."

Ben laughed, and Chloe realized she would miss the sound.

"Well, if that's what this is, then I should tell you it's been a pleasure being married to you."

The seriousness in Ben's voice made Chloe's throat feel a little tight. "Yeah, well, just remember you said that when my lawyer's suing for half your stuff," she joked.

Her reward was a crooked smile, but it kind of hurt to look at it, and she found she had to avert her eyes.

"Ma'am?" The doorman's voice intruded in the nick of time. "Your taxi has arrived."

"Guess that's my cue." She motioned toward the waiting car with a tip of her head.

"What? Oh, yeah. Here, let me." Ben beat her to the suitcase—as always—and they walked the few steps through the door and onto the sidewalk, stopping beside the car. "Did you want this in the trunk?" he asked, and she shook her head.

"Nah. It can ride with me."

He set it down on the snowy sidewalk.

A moment passed as they just stared at each other, their shoulders hunched against the wind.

"Okay, well, 'bye," she said, at the same time he said, "Chloe, I just—"

They both snapped their mouths closed.

"You just what?" she asked. Her heartbeat tripled its pace, at least.

He glanced at her suitcase, then back at her. "Um, have a good flight, okay? It was… It was really nice meeting you."

"Yeah." Her nod was forceful. "It was nice meeting you, too," she said, meaning it so deeply that she had to mask her disappointment with a bright smile. And then she kind of went in for a hug, and he kind of went in for a hug, and they were hugging awkwardly. Chloe knew she held on just a little too long, but she couldn't help it.

Ben returned her plastic smile with one of his own as he grabbed the handle and pulled the cab door open. She wanted to say something to him, something more, but she had no idea what—Keep in touch? Wanna hook up again sometime? Thanks for the orgasms? I'm really going to miss you?

All that came out was "Thanks." Then she folded herself inside the warm but slightly worn interior of the taxi.

Ben placed her suitcase on the floor beside her, and rested one hand on the top of the car and the other on the door, so he could duck his head in enough to make eye contact.

"Goodbye, Chloe Masterson."

His smile was sad and genuine, and knowing she'd never see it again made her chest feel fuzzy.

She did her best to return the smile, and Chloe hated that hers felt a little wobbly, but she managed to say, "Goodbye, Ben Masterson," and give him enough time to close the door before her stupid tear ducts betrayed her.

# 8

WHEN BEN WALKED into his office on Monday morning, he was greeted by hearty congratulations and back slaps and a bottle of laudatory wine on his desk from Carson and McLeod. Well, it was probably from one of their admin assistants since the card was electronically signed, but still.

He was proud of landing the account, of course, but since he'd been home, he couldn't drum up the excitement that he usually held for a new challenge.

Ben took a seat at his desk and looked around his office—the same dove-gray walls, the same black-and-white photos of Seattle architecture, the same glass-and-chrome accents—and he was struck by how colorless his existence had become.

There'd been a time when he'd been proud of his job. At thirty, he was already a team lead, and with any luck, being seriously considered for the promotion to account director. He should be on top of the world right now, but he couldn't shake the way Chloe had correctly pegged him in three seconds flat. It was making him doubt the paint-by-numbers progression of his life.

Where was the excitement? The spontaneity?

Smothered, no doubt, by a series of five-year plans. Get a degree. Get a job. Get promoted. He'd Stalin-ized his life into a bland progression of what he'd once thought were bigger and better goals. And now he had a great job, sure, but was that all he had?

When was the last time he'd hung out with his friends? His once-weekly basketball game with his best friend, Oz, had become sporadic at best, and it scared him that work had taken over his whole life. But wasn't that what it took to realize big goals?

"Ben?"

He glanced up, managing a smile for his team's admin assistant. He noticed that in contrast to her patterned dress, her makeup was subdued. "Hey, Lana. How was your weekend?"

"Not as great as yours! Congratulations on landing the Burke account. It's all anyone is talking about around here. In fact, you've just been summoned to Carson's office. Better get a move on," she advised. "I have a feeling it's good news."

He nodded, getting to his feet.

"Lana, what do you think of this suit?" He motioned at himself. Her eyes tracked down his navy jacket—the one Chloe had called boring—his white shirt and his striped tie.

"Looks great, boss," she assured him. Then she added, "Just like always."

And that, Ben decided, heading for the elevator, was the problem.

The silver doors slid open almost immediately, and he stepped inside, hitting the button for the top floor. It wasn't until he was striding toward his boss's office that he realized he'd been humming a Neil Diamond song.

"Good morning, Ben. They're expecting you."

"Thanks, Doris." He nodded as he strode past the reception desk toward the imposing glass door. Ben straightened his lapels and stepped inside.

"Ben!" Rob Carson's booming voice greeted him. The heavyset man stood and extended a meaty hand in Ben's direction.

"Mr. Carson." Ben reached across the imposing desk and shook his hand. He then turned to the thin, bespectacled man standing in front of the other black leather visitor's chair. "Mr. McLeod," he said, accepting the man's hand in a shake that was much more reserved.

Rob Carson and Hugh McLeod couldn't be more different in looks, in demeanor, or in sheer decibels, but they were completely in sync when it came to the business of advertising.

"Thank you both for the wine. I appreciate the gesture."

"Well deserved, Ben, well deserved. Please, have a seat. Hugh and I just wanted to say congratulations on a job well done! We just got off the phone with Burke, and he's raving about you. Raving!"

"I'm glad he feels the meeting went as well as I do. I appreciate you taking a chance and sending me. I think Hotel Burke will be a great addition to our company portfolio."

"Indeed it will. We do have another matter to discuss with you," McLeod added in his eerily calm way.

"Oh?" Ben's palms prickled, a precursor to sweat. *This is it!* The promotion he'd been waiting for. The raise meant he could finally buy the lakefront cabin he had his eye on. The one he and his dad used to fish near. It was all coming together. Just like he'd planned.

Carson was smiling, a big, gaping grin. "Turns out you're not the only one the old man was raving about."

"Oh?" Ben said again. The noncommittal syllable was all he could muster.

*Son of a...* Who else had been talking to Burke? He'd thought he had the account all locked up.

"Seems he was also very taken with your wife," McLeod informed him.

Ben gripped the black leather armrests to steady himself, but his slick hands slid right off.

"What's with the secret-keeping? How come you didn't tell us you got married, Ben?" Carson's booming voice sounded even louder than usual to Ben's ears. "I mean, I know we're your bosses, but I was practically your father-in-law for a few years there. Melanie was almost as surprised as me when I mentioned you'd gotten yourself hitched!"

*He told Melanie?*

"It's great news, though. The kind of thing that can really help you get to the next level here. Stability is good for business. But you've been working like a madman, lately. When did you have a chance to strap on the ol' ball and chain?"

So many expletives, so little time.

"Oh, it's all pretty recent," he managed to answer. Ben tugged at his tie. Man, it was hot in this office. "I like to keep my business life and my personal life separate. Keep my focus on the work." There. That sounded pretty good, didn't it?

"Admirable," said McLeod, "but nonsense. We'd love to meet your bride."

"Definitely! This could be the dawn of a new era for you here at Carson and McLeod! You know we're looking for a new account director. With the work ethic you've exhibited over the last while, we've put you on the short list, Ben."

It should have been great news. It *was* great news. Unfortunately, Ben couldn't fully enjoy it, because the great news also came with a great big catch.

"We're setting up dinner parties with all the candidates so Hugh and I can come to your home, meet the family, get a real sense of who will be the best fit for the upper-management team. Plus, it's a great test run. Advertising is a very social world, and we want to see what will happen when we set you loose with our big clients. We've got you penciled in to host next Saturday. It's the perfect opportunity to meet this wife of yours."

*I am so. Damn. Screwed.*

"How does that sound, Benny?"

*Awful. Just the worst.*

"Good. So good." Ben swiped his hand across his forehead, smearing the droplets of sweat trickling down from his hairline.

"Excellent! You can get the details about food allergies and who will be attending from Doris on your way out. Stellar work this weekend, Ben. Hugh and I see great things in your future."

Somehow Ben managed to get to his feet, make it through another round of handshakes and book it out of the office.

With the envelope full of dinner party instructions Doris had given him clutched in his fist, Ben began the long trip back to his desk.

Meanwhile in his head he reviewed the past five promotions awarded. Every single recipient had been married. How had he never noticed that before?

Ben shut the door behind him when he got back to his office and collapsed into his chair.

He was screwed. And not the good kind.

He scrubbed his hands over his face. "Okay, Masterson, think. There's a way out of this. You just have to figure out what it is."

After a long few minutes, he finally picked up the phone and got Lana on the line.

"What can I do for you, boss?"

"I, uh. Well, I was just sort of…wondering, really…" *Oh for God's sake!* "Where do you buy your makeup?"

There was a moment of silence on the other end of the line. "I'm sorry?"

Ben pinched the bridge of his nose between his thumb and index finger. He had a headache coming on. "Is there a store you go to? One that sells face stuff?"

The line went dead. Ben hung up the receiver.

*And three, two, one…*

"What is going on?" Lana burst through his door, right on cue, practically slamming it closed in her haste to get to the gray leather visitor's chair on the other side of his desk. "Why do you want to know where I buy my makeup? Oh, my God. Are you trying to buy someone a present? Do you have a girlfriend you haven't told me about?"

"No. Lana, I don't have a girlfriend."

Her eyes lit with understanding and she lowered her voice conspiratorially. "Is it for you?"

"What? No!"

She shrugged. "Okay. That's too bad. I've always secretly wondered how you'd look in drag. So spill, then. It's not for a girlfriend, and it's not for you. What am I missing?"

"I met this woman—"

"Aha!"

Ben frowned.

"Sorry. Continue."

"I met her, and now I need to track her down. And all I know is that she sells makeup at a store in the mall."

"Which mall?"

"I have no idea."

"This is potentially the greatest thing I've ever gotten to do in all my time working at Carson and McLeod. You call the boutique shops, I'll take the department stores." She grabbed his notepad and pen and scribbled down five store names for him and handed it back. "What's her name?"

"Chloe Masterson."

"Masterson?"

"It's a long story."

When it became obvious he was not going to elaborate further, Lana crossed her arms over her chest. "If we find her, you owe me an explanation, boss."

"You've got yourself a deal."

Thirty-five minutes later, Ben was not quite so optimistic about Lana's chances of cashing in on their deal.

Ben tossed his pen on the desk and plowed his fingers through his hair. He missed the good old days when everyone had a landline that was listed in the phone book.

A glance at the clock let him know he'd managed to accomplish no work in the two hours that had passed since he'd arrived at the office. He looked back at the Post-it Lana had left with him. He was going to have so much work to catch up on tomorrow. With a sigh, he typed *Titanium Beauty* into Google, clicked on store locations, and started his next round of calls.

IT WAS FOUR O'CLOCK by the time Ben finally made it to the mall, and another ten minutes before he found Titanium Beauty. He'd ultimately located it by following a horde of high school girls.

Titanium Beauty was packed with bodies, and he was

having a tough time figuring out if one of them was Chloe's.

The guy on the phone had said she'd be here, so Ben continued to look, leaning back and to the right for a better view of the tills. He almost toppled over when he caught sight of a woman with a choppy black bob with stoplight-red highlights shot through it standing behind the register. Someone with berry-stained lips and green-gold eyes.

*Chloe.*

Not that he was surprised to see her. Obviously. He'd come here for exactly that reason. But he was shocked at how different she seemed. She looked more comfortable, more in control—and smoking hot.

She was *so* kick-ass-animé-heroine hot, in fact, that Ben was having trouble believing she was the same woman who'd cried on his shoulder in a midlevel hotel room. Ben couldn't move his gaze away from her as the line inched forward.

He'd put so much effort into the "finding" part of the plan that he didn't have a contingency for the "talking" part. He had no idea what to say to her. A fact that became painfully obvious when he finally made it to the front of the line and all he could do was grin at her like a moron.

She turned to the next person in line.

"Welcome to Titanium Beauty, did you find everything you— Oh, my God! Ben! What are you doing here?"

His beautifully crooked smile made her heart lurch in her chest.

"Man, I'd hate to hear how you greet the guys you're *not* married to."

Josh's head whipped in her direction. Honest to God,

when it came to gossip her best friend had the ears of a bat.

"Listen, Ben." She tried to keep her voice normal so as not to draw any more of Josh's attention, all the while pleading with her eyes. "Now's really not a good time, and—"

"You're married?" Josh interrupted.

"Nope." *Nothing to see here, Josh. Move along.* "I'm working right now, Masterson."

She winced internally at her blunder.

"You just called him 'Masterson.' That's *your* last name."

"Yes, Josh. We got married, and he changed his last name to mine. We both wore pants. Ben's very into female equality. He's a real suffragette's wet dream." She flicked her attention back to Ben. "Can we talk later?"

Josh shot her a look that confirmed he was questioning her mental health. "He just said he's your husband."

"Inside joke," she bit out. She loved Josh, but he was irrepressible when it came to hooking his friends up. It had taken her three months to get him to stop trying to fix her up with the new guy at the sporting-goods store next to Titanium Beauty. She didn't need him hounding her about Ben. She was having a tough enough time keeping the adman out of her thoughts as it was.

"Actually, it's kind of a funny story," Ben began charmingly, and Chloe wanted to kick him in the shin. If not for the counter in her way, she would have. "We got stranded together in Chicago last week when our plane broke down."

*Shut up, Ben.*

"You went to Chicago last week?" Josh demanded. "I thought you were going to Buffalo for your sister's wedding!"

"Actually, we were both headed to Buffalo. But there was this big snowstorm and we ended up sharing a hotel room—"

*Oh. God. No.*

Chloe closed her eyes. She could feel Josh's excitement mounting over this new love match.

Finally, *mercifully*, Ben shut up. "Chloe? What's the matter? Are you okay?" he asked, placing a comforting hand on her arm. The show of concern made her feel like even more of an ass.

"Actually, Chloe's been a bit under the weather, haven't you, Chloe?" Josh barged behind the counter and shoved her out of the way. "You should probably take her to the food court so you two can talk while she rehydrates with a smoothie. I'll take over on cash. Bring me back a banana-mango."

"I'll only be five minutes," she told Josh.

He waved her off. "Five minutes, an hour. Whatever. Take your time."

She grabbed Ben by one big strong arm and tugged him out of the store and into the mall, whirling to face him.

*I missed you.*

The unbidden thought took her completely by surprise.

"Ben, what are you doing here?"

*It's really good to see you. You're just as hot as I remembered.* She crossed her arms over her chest, trying to resist her shameless hormones. *Be strong, Chloe.*

"I'm in the middle of a shift."

"I know." He nodded. "*I know.* And I'm so sorry to bother you at work, but I've run into a slight predicament, and the thing is, Chloe, I need you."

*Well, dammit.* She didn't stand a chance.

# 9

"SO, THIS IS IT. Welcome home."

Chloe stepped in front of Ben and through the door. "Wow."

Sand-colored walls, dark wood flooring and pristine white crown molding combined with Ben's total lack of kitsch—or anything even remotely personal—completed the illusion that she was touring a swanky show home.

"It's like you live in a catalog."

Something flickered in Ben's amber eyes—hurt?—but he turned to shut the door and when he faced her again, his easy smile was in full bloom.

"A nice catalog, though, right? From one of those up-scale stores?"

"Definitely a nice one," she agreed, figuring that he didn't need to know "nice" was code for bland. Besides, who was she to judge? Her apartment was serviceable and clean, but it wouldn't be scoring a magazine spread any time soon. She'd bet you could barely hear the pipes or the neighbors' TV in a place like this. "How long have you lived here?"

"A year and a half." He threw his keys on the kitchen counter—granite, natch—and pulled his black peacoat off. He hung it in the small closet to their right, then did the same with Chloe's.

*A year and a half*? She'd have been less surprised if he'd said yesterday. *Spartan* was too kind a description.

"Want a tour?" he offered, picking up her suitcase.

"Lead the way."

"Okay, let's see. Kitchen." He pointed to the left. In addition to the granite, Chloe saw what she expected to see in a high-class condo: galley style, open concept and lots of stainless steel. "Living room." High ceilings, a sectional and a man-size television. "Bathroom." Glass-encased mega shower with rainfall showerhead. "Office-slash-second-bedroom." She wasn't even paying attention anymore. At least not until he stopped in front of the last door on the tour.

"And this, this is where the magic happens."

"If you have a waterbed, I'm outta here."

Ben grinned as they stepped inside and he set her suitcase on the dark hardwood floor. "Obviously, as my guest, you can pick which side of the bed you want."

Chloe walked over to the big bed and pushed on the end of the mattress, relieved that it didn't slosh. "Why choose when you'll be sleeping on the couch?" she said sweetly.

He leaned a shoulder against the door frame, crossing his arms.

Was he actually handsomer here in Seattle, or was it her imagination?

"My house, my rules."

"Come on now, sweetie. Don't you mean *our* house?"

"You'd really make me spend our honeymoon on the couch? Even though we've already slept together?" He shot her a sexy half smile and added, "Twice."

*Ha.* As if she could forget. In fact, she had a sneaking suspicion it was the driving force behind her decision to agree to this ridiculous scheme of his. Her brain had tried to reason with her lady parts, but they weren't having any of her logic.

"Yeah, but that was back when we were strangers. We're married now. According to all sitcoms in the history of the world, that means sex is just a distant memory for us."

"Aw, man!" He reached for his wallet and pulled out the ring. "I'm not sure I want to give this to you anymore."

Truthfully, neither did she. Chloe had spent their weekend apart replaying every X-rated moment of their nights together. Their fake relationship had affected her more deeply than she'd realized. How was she going to deal with more? But even as she thought it, she heard herself say, "Then why don't you put that away and tell me what you *do* want."

Her brazen invitation lit a dangerous glint in his whiskey eyes. Chloe licked her lips, unable to speak as he shoved the ring in the pocket of his jeans and started toward her.

Ben was on the prowl, and it was sexy as hell. He reached for the hem of his shirt, pulling it over his head as he stalked closer. By the time he stood before her, so close that she could feel the heat rolling off his body, Chloe was so turned on she could barely breathe.

Oh, God. This. This was what she'd wanted from the moment she'd lifted her gaze from the cash register to find him standing there.

She raised her arms so he could tug her T-shirt up and off, and he growled his approval as she reached behind her. The purple demi-cup went slack. She tugged the bra the rest of the way off, dropping it where it fell. Their wordless striptease continued in tandem, as they slowly divested themselves of their jeans and underwear, then stood to face each other.

"Please tell me that was enough foreplay, because I'm going to explode if I don't get inside you right now."

Chloe moaned her agreement and the next thing she knew, they were on the bed and his weight was pressing into her everywhere but where she needed him most. She rocked her hips against him.

"Jesus. Hold on. Condom," he said, crawling over to the end table.

She was impressed at how quickly he managed the task at hand. Then he was back on top of her and she was so wet, so ready for him. They both groaned with satisfaction as he entered her, and she raised her knees to make sure he was as far in as possible.

"I thought this would never happen again," he confessed against her neck, and he thrust inside her so deep and so slow that she couldn't form the words "same here" through the pleasure that was speeding through her veins like liquid fire. She wound her legs around his hips, urging him to go harder and faster, and he obliged.

She'd never gotten this hot this quickly. Already a familiar tingle was growing low in her belly, and she knew she was close.

"Make me come, Ben," she pleaded, and he plunged into her so forcefully that she gasped with delight. She dug her fingernails into his back as the orgasm hit, sharp and fast. The whole world came apart and only Ben's weight pressing her into the mattress kept her together.

She'd never had a quickie before, but if that's what they were like, she definitely would be having one again. Long and drawn-out had its charms, but she'd never felt anything quite as intense as what had just happened between them.

Ben rolled off her and they both lay in the tangle of sheets, staring at the ceiling, trying to catch their breath. With her hormones sated and no longer clouding her thoughts, Chloe realized things were starting to feel real. Terrifyingly real.

What were they even thinking? Who was going to believe their lies in such a permanent setting? This wasn't a quick breakfast with a stranger. This was dinner at his house with his bosses. People who'd known the real Ben for years and saw him on a daily basis.

"Ben, I'm not sure I can do this," she blurted, imploring him to understand.

"Too late," he joked. He rolled onto his stomach, his entire side pressing against hers as he lowered his beautiful face close to hers.

She didn't like the way her resolve waned in direct proportion to his nearness. The earlier desire to run had been replaced with something else. Something dangerous. The part of her that wanted to stay.

"What I mean," she stressed, "is maybe it's not such a good idea, me staying here."

"I thought we decided you moving in here was the best chance we had to learn enough about each other to pass as a happily married couple on Saturday."

"We did, but—"

"I also thought we decided that this was the easiest way to make sure you have a presence in the house so that a casual observer would believe my wife has been living with me for whatever undetermined amount of time it's been since we got married."

"I know, but—"

"I'm not Patrick, Chloe. This is you and me. Just like

before. We've got each other's backs. No matter what."
The words, spoken like a vow, stole her breath.

"Besides, it's not as if any of this is real," he reminded
her.

The sting of truth pulled her out of her spiral of panic.
Chloe nodded. "You're right. Okay, I'm in."

Ben looked at her. "You're in?"

"I'll stay."

"That's just… Okay, then. Great." His smile was boy-
ish. He leaned off the side of the bed for a moment,
and then flopped down beside her. When he raised his
hand, his grandmother's wedding ring glinted between
his thumb and index finger.

With only a tremor of trepidation, Chloe took the ring
from him. Ben was right. He wasn't Patrick. And she
wasn't the scared twenty-two-year-old who'd fled down
the aisle and across the country.

As she slid the ring back onto her finger, she made
a vow to herself. She was going to stick this out until
Saturday, no matter what. Ben needed her help, and she
wasn't going to run out on him.

## 10

BEN FINISHED BUTTONING the cuffs of his white dress shirt and grabbed the gray suit jacket off the hanger. It was the same suit he'd been wearing on the plane when he'd met Chloe, but by the time that had occurred to him, he was already half-dressed. Besides, changing his pants would have felt too much like an acknowledgment that his clothing choice this morning might not have been completely random.

Ben glanced at his watch. He needed to hurry if he was going to make it to the office for seven. He had a lot of work to catch up on since he'd sacrificed most of yesterday to hunting Chloe down. His beeline for the door was interrupted by a beautiful woman sporting bed-head, perfectly applied makeup and a ratty blue Vote for Nixon T-shirt. Obviously meant for a stout, 1972 Republican, it hit her just past midthigh.

"You want breakfast?" she asked, shaking a box of cereal toward him. "I think, after years of tinkering, I have finally found an ambrosia-like ratio of honey to nut."

He smiled at the quip. "I'd love to, Chloe. I would. But part of the reason I'm so good at my job is that I get there by seven every morning."

"Just stay for ten minutes? I was kind of hoping we could talk about this dinner on Saturday. There's a ton of stuff that goes into hosting the perfect business dinner, and besides being good at your job, you've got none of them. Trust me when I tell you, I've learned from the master. And my mother has passed those tips and tricks on to me, because I had no say in the matter."

For the first time since he'd set his sights on this promotion a year and a half ago, he wanted to stay home and plan a dinner party. The fact that he was even considering it shook him, and gave his words an edge. "I don't really have ten minutes to spare for this right now."

Chloe set the box on the counter. "Oh. Okay." He could read the hurt in her expressive eyes as she poured milk into her bowl.

Ben managed a smile, an attempt to numb the sting. "I'll see you later, though." He grabbed his coat from the hall closet and jammed his socked feet into the square-toed dress shoes he'd left by the door.

"Way later. I'm closing tonight. Josh's band has a gig so I told him I'd cover his shift. I should be back around eleven."

He glanced over as Chloe appeared, her shoulder resting against the doorway to the kitchen, one bare foot curled over the other as she ate her cereal standing up.

"Have a good day," she said.

Ben's chest constricted a little at the wifely sentiment, but he couldn't say why.

He stepped toward her and she stopped chewing, her spoon frozen in her hand. He was too close. He knew it, but he couldn't bring himself to move. She smelled warm and sensual, but with an edge. Like vanilla laced with bourbon.

Ben swallowed, reaching behind her to grab his keys

off the counter. It was all he could do not to brush a soft kiss to her flushed cheek. Her lips.

He wanted to tug off that hideous T-shirt and see what she was—or wasn't—wearing underneath. Push her up against the granite countertop or the stainless-steel fridge. Touch her everywhere.

*Masochist*, he chided himself, taking a big step away from temptation. "See you tonight, Chloe." He didn't look back as he pulled the door shut behind him.

IT WAS AFTER nine when Ben pulled his truck into the condo's underground parking that night. He'd caught up on all his work and even used his supper break to squeeze in a quick workout. Despite the productive day, he still had a few things to finish up, and he grabbed his tablet as he sat down on the couch. But he couldn't concentrate. He was acutely aware of how empty the condo felt tonight.

Stupid, since until yesterday he'd lived here alone for a year and a half and never realized how quiet it was before. He could only attribute the weird sensation to the fact that Chloe had left reminders of herself everywhere. A pair of heels tipped over at the door, a dirty mug in the sink. Her notebook and a makeup magazine on the coffee table. The duvet from his bed jammed in the corner of the couch, like the empty husk of a cocoon after the butterfly had flown away.

He ran a frustrated hand across his hair. He *really* needed to get a handle on Hotel Burke's website and familiarize himself with the analytics before he met with his team the next morning. But the siren song of YouTube kept tempting him, trying to make him do the thing he'd been trying not to do for days.

She'd hate it.

He knew she'd hate it.

But he was dying to check out her makeup channel. And she wasn't home yet. She never had to know, he reasoned. The argument was convincing enough that he swiped back to his home screen and opened the You-Tube app.

He typed "makeup" and "Chloe" into the search field and with one tap of his finger, his screen was filled with thumbnails of her, dozens of them, spanning several different hair colors and so many combinations of makeup that Ben's mind was blown.

Pink-lipped Chloe, red-lipped Chloe, Chloe with eyeliner, Chloe with no eyeliner, Chloe looking sweet, Chloe looking sultry, Chloe looking tough—he couldn't even fathom that the mess of brushes and bottles and powders littering the bathroom counter right now could be responsible for all of them.

He scrolled through the page. Most of the videos had thumbnails with the same background—probably her bedroom at home, but he found himself clicking on the poorly-lit one at the very top of the page. The most recent one.

The video loaded, and there she was. She might as well have been a different person with her hair a uniform brown. Now that he'd met the real Chloe, the smart, strong woman who lived life on her own terms, he had a hard time remembering he'd known her before her hair was black and red.

"Hi, guys, Chloe here. I'm on the road this week, and as you can see my accommodations are not the most glamorous, but that's no reason not to look like a million bucks!"

Ben was mesmerized by the process as Chloe transformed herself into the stormy-eyed goddess who'd done all kinds of naughty things with him on the quiltless bed behind her left shoulder.

But the video wasn't compelling just because her sex appeal was off the Richter scale, or because he had intimate knowledge of the black satin bra he remembered was hiding under that T-shirt. Chloe was actually a really good teacher. Despite her tendency toward sarcasm and privacy in real life, onscreen her demeanor was very open and relaxed. She was a dynamic speaker, not plagued by the "ums" and "likes" that peppered most people's diction when asked to wing it on camera. And even with the shitty lighting in the Value Inn, it was clear that she loved what she was doing.

There was true passion behind her words and the way she applied her makeup. He'd been more right on the plane than he'd realized. Chloe *was* an artist.

He clicked around a bit, watched more snippets of her videos. He couldn't find a single one, though, where she didn't start with all her foundation and one eye already done. He realized he'd never seen her without any makeup on.

Sometimes she did investigative-type videos, showing the advertising claims of the product and how they didn't work as shown, before giving some tips on how to achieve the product's promise through alternate means. Even though she basically called out his entire profession in them, these videos were his favorites—especially the one about something called "lip plumpers" because she was particularly scathing in it. After a while, though, the strategic part of his brain took over, and he became obsessed with the metrics.

She'd been making videos for about eight months, yet her subscriber list was much lower than he'd have suspected. Especially considering that at least a third of her thirty-two videos showed a dramatic upswing of comments and views over the last week. He couldn't be sure, but judging by the comments, it seemed as if talking to Kenley Burke had paid major dividends. Imagine if she told even a few friends about the site. And if each of them told a few friends…

Even without the word of mouth, some of Chloe's special-event tutorials—like Halloween and New Year's Eve—were fast approaching ten thousand hits. Those were the kinds of numbers that would push her revenue into higher brackets.

But what amazed him the most was her total lack of self-promotion. She had no social media accounts linked to her channel, no website. Her entire reach was organic—makeup-wearers of all ages, from all over the world, stumbling across Chloe's videos by sheer luck and then sharing them with their friends.

But by not linking to the products she was using, she was leaving thousands of dollars' worth of affiliate money on the table. She needed to up the quality of her videos, too. Nothing some decent lighting and a new laptop wouldn't fix.

With only a bare minimum of work, Chloe could turn her hobby into an empire. He was sure of it.

Ben's heart rate picked up. He was having that moment again. The electric rush that came when his brain churned with ideas. He could help her transform Makeup by Chloe into something even bigger and better than it was now.

The sound of her key in the door startled him and he panicked. He hit the button to switch off his screen and shoved the tablet on the coffee table, exchanging it for the makeup magazine she'd left there. He settled into the couch and aimed for nonchalance.

CHLOE PUSHED HER way into the condo, kicking off her blister-producing high heels as she shut the door and locked it. God, it was good to be home. She headed straight for the fridge, dropping her purse on the counter and yanking a tub of Phish Food from the freezer.

"Ben?" she called, opening the cutlery drawer.

"In here," came the reply, and she snagged two spoons before bumping the drawer shut with her hip and heading into the living room.

Ben was sprawled comfortably on the couch, his bare feet crossed at the ankles and propped up on the coffee table. He was wearing a white T-shirt and gray sweats. And to top off the cuteness that was Ben, he wasn't watching TV. He was reading.

She raised her eyebrows as she took in exactly *what* he was reading, and he blushed when he closed the worn magazine and tossed it onto the table beside his tablet. "So, how'd it go today?"

"Well," Chloe began, dropping onto the cushion beside him. Her shoulder pressed against his upper arm.

"Work itself was okay." She mimicked his relaxed, feet-on-coffee-table position and pulled the top off the frozen nectar of the dairy gods. She gave him a spoon and Ben dug in before she'd dropped the lid on the cushion beside her.

"What do you call your penis?" she asked, and Ben's other hand flew to his mouth, ostensibly to keep his behemoth spoonful of ice cream from falling off his tongue.

Chloe dug a chocolate fish from the pint with her spoon and let it melt on her tongue. "Have you given it a name? You know, something you call it when you're with a special lady? Like Excalibur or Big Ben?"

She couldn't help that her eyes darted covertly to his crotch. If she remembered correctly—and she did—

either of those names were appropriate. Oh, geez! Chloe hunched her shoulders, hoping her nipples wouldn't betray her gutter mind.

Clearing her throat, she pressed on. "Or are you into more generic innuendo? Like, 'Hey, baby. I've got a package for you'?"

Ben's face was scrunched up with disgust, which she found kind of endearing. "I'm trying to eat here," he protested. "Why are you talking about dicks?"

Chloe dragged her spoon delicately along the top of the ice cream until she had a perfect curl. "Because the creepy delivery guy who dropped off our new Valentine's Day signage asked if I wanted to go in the back room—"

"Jesus, did he try anything? Are you okay?"

Chloe was taken aback by Ben's sudden intensity. "I'm fine. That's why I'm trying to tell you the funny story of what happened to me today."

He stared at her for a long moment before his muscles relaxed.

"What's going on with you?"

Ben shook his head. "Nothing."

She gave him a hard look to let him know she wasn't buying it.

"It's nothing. Finish your story. He wanted you to go into the back room…" he prodded.

"Because he wanted me to play with his *trouser snake*."

Ben froze. "He did not say that."

"I swear on Ben and Jerry's lives."

They stared at one another for a moment in shared horror before bursting into laughter.

"So if you have some cutesy name for your lower anatomy, I need to know now. Because I discovered something important about myself tonight—I can't live with a man who says things like that."

"I don't. But for the record, after that speech, I wouldn't tell you even if I did."

Chloe smiled. "For fear of constant and merciless mocking? Or because you don't want me to leave?" she asked, putting her spoon in her mouth upside-down, applying the ice cream directly to her tongue.

Ben sobered and glanced over at her. The smile slipped from her lips as awareness hummed between them. Her nipples tingled as she slipped the spoon from her mouth and forced herself to swallow. "Okay, seriously though," she said, barging through the moment in the interest of self-preservation. He'd been kind of a jerk to her at breakfast. She was not going to fall right into bed with him. "What's your penis's name? Because I feel like that's something a wife would know. What if your boss asks?"

Ben took her cue, dispelling the remainder of the tension with a grin. "I like your moxie, Masterson. You're taking this seriously, preparing for every eventuality."

"A good hostess always has a bevy of conversation topics at her disposal."

"Yes, she does. And speaking of conversation topics, I have something I need to tell you."

Chloe went still at the serious note in his voice.

"I watched some of your makeup videos."

"What?" The blood drained from her face. It was like she'd been soul-jacked. A ridiculous reaction, she knew, since she'd posted her soul on YouTube herself.

"They're great. You're very natural on camera."

"Thanks."

Ben laughed. "Your words say 'thank you' but your tone says 'fuck you, Ben.'"

That was probably true .

"I just do it for fun."

"I think that's your first mistake. Makeup by Chloe has the potential to be a big deal. It could be a brick and mortar business—I mean, you did your sister's wedding makeup for free, obviously, but people pay big money for that. Or you can keep the business online. If you write anything like you speak in those videos, you could branch into a blog and it could lead to sponsorships, or just new audiences. You could even do a little of both, kind of dovetail them together, depending on your vision."

Ben's lecture was starting to feel like the speech her dad had given her before she applied for law school. "You will do this and you will go here." Before she'd realized it, all her choices had been taken away.

She knew Ben was just trying to help. That his suggestions came from a good place, but…Makeup by Chloe was hers. And Ben didn't have the right to make these decisions for her. That was the whole reason she'd started her YouTube channel in the first place.

"… I mean, just talking with Kenley resulted in a huge spike in your numbers. Imagine if—"

"Hey, Ben?"

"Yeah?"

"I don't want to talk about this anymore."

"Right, I know, I'm getting ahead of myself, but it's not as intimidating as it sounds. Even just linking to the products you use could result in an impressive amount of affiliate revenue and—"

"Ben!"

He started at her brusque tone.

"I said I don't want to talk about it."

"Fine. I get it." His voice belied his words. He wasn't happy. She'd hurt his feelings.

*Well, join the club.*

"I've got some work to finish up anyway. I'll be in the office."

"Okay." It was all she could say as she watched him leave.

It wasn't that she didn't feel badly about cutting him off. He talked a good game. Made her consider things she usually dismissed as fanciful. But Makeup by Chloe wasn't ready yet. She wasn't prepared to put it out in the world until she learned more techniques, and saved more money. Until she felt like a businesswoman, not an imposter. Doing makeup made her happy, sure, but she had so much more to prove before people would pay for her services. Before she could really make use of his advice.

She looked down at the ice cream in her hand. It had melted a fair bit during their chat. She put the lid back on it and headed into the kitchen to put it away, dropping her and Ben's spoons in the sink as she passed by.

It was only the second night since he'd tracked her down, but they'd already started fighting and stopped having sex. Real life was intruding on their fantasy more quickly than she'd expected.

## 11

CHLOE DIPPED HER roller into the blue-gray paint and rolled a trial stripe of it onto the wall, excited at how well everything was coming together.

It hadn't started out that way.

Ben had already left for work by the time Chloe got up. After last night, it felt odd being alone in his place. She wasn't sure if it was the residual effect of their sorta-fight or just the inherent emptiness of the condo, but it had to change. Fast. They were only days away from the business dinner that could make or break Ben's career.

And right now it looked like they were faking their entire relationship. Well, except for the sex. No faking required there. But orgasms weren't the kind of proof they needed. As things stood, no one would walk into this empty bachelor pad and believe a happy couple lived here. Hell, she barely believed Ben lived here.

Ben didn't think redecorating was important. He thought saying he had a wife was enough to convey stability, but Chloe knew better.

She might have rebelled against that life, but she was intimately familiar with the world of business dinners. It was all about appearances, about projecting a certain lifestyle. Every detail said something about what was happening inside a house.

Ben didn't understand that yet, but he was going to when he saw the magic she'd worked today.

It had started with the modest hope of finding somewhere in the condo a throw for the couch or a photo for the wall—anything that would loan his place a little hominess. Instead, she'd found a trunk full of amazing stuff just sitting out in the open in Ben's makeshift office.

It had contained a few fishing trophies that she'd displayed beside the TV, a homemade quilt in shades of blue that she'd draped over the back of his couch, and her favorite find—a bunch of incredible pictures from Ben's youth.

She couldn't decide which one of the photos she loved best. The one of a young Ben and his dad fishing at a beautiful lake with an amazing log cabin in the background, the picture of the two of them making faces at the camera from the box of a beat-up red pickup truck, or another of a teenaged Ben in his cap and gown with his father's arm around him and pride shining in the man's eyes.

That's when she'd decided to go all out, because these beautiful memories deserved a room that suited them. She'd picked up some paint for a feature wall in the living room and an inexpensive bookcase that she'd assembled herself. She'd even swung by her place for a couple of throw pillows, some books, a box of candles, and a few framed pictures of her and her friends to add to the mix and help sell the illusion.

She set the roller back in the tray and took in the rest of the room while she waited for her test patch to dry.

She was proud of how much personality she'd imbued

in the room for a mere sixty-seven dollars and a couple of hours of her time.

And once she finished painting this feature wall, she could hang a few more photos and they would have a hope in hell of convincing his bosses that this relationship wasn't a sham.

Ben might be the ultimate ad exec, but if being raised by Fiona Masterson had taught her anything, it was how to be the woman behind the man.

And everyone knew that was the important part.

"CHLOE? I'M HOME, and I've got pizza!"

Ben's meeting had gone really well and he'd managed to tie up things at the office more quickly than he'd anticipated. It was only seven o'clock and he was already done for the day.

The door had barely shut behind him before he was struck by two things: the distinct chill in the apartment and the unmistakable smell of paint.

Chloe glanced over her shoulder, and pulled the bud from her ear. "Sorry. Music." She removed the other earbud. "Didn't hear you come in. Surprise!"

Ben walked right into the middle of the room, the pizza forgotten in his hands. "That is…blue. Like, blue-blue. I'm talking *really* blue."

"You've got a real way with words, Masterson. You should write poetry in your spare time. Flight attendants the world over will swoon. More than they already do, that is."

"Why are you painting my wall blue?"

"It's not blue, it's *arctic mist*."

"Why are you painting my wall arctic mist?"

"Because it's going to look great." Chloe set her roller in the paint tray and turned to face him. "This is an intervention. I'm trying to save you. I mean, I consider it a miracle that you haven't shriveled up and died of beige yet!"

His eyes flitted through the room, barely able to track all the changes. "Where did you get my grandmother's quilt? And my dad's fishing trophies?"

Then he caught sight of his graduation photo. On a bookshelf he'd never seen before. "What have you done?"

Chloe looked taken aback. "I redecorated."

"What the hell for?"

She frowned. "This is what I wanted to talk to you about over breakfast yesterday. Your bosses are never going to believe we're married."

"Sure they will. A lot of people already do."

"Right, but we were out. Maybe they'd believe us if we were having the dinner at a restaurant. But they're coming *here*," she said in a tone that suggested he'd just been checkmated in the argument.

"So?"

"So? This is not the house of a happy couple, Ben. It's the house of a robot. You have a couch, a TV and a gaming console. Even frat boys put up some pictures of naked ladies making out!"

"That still doesn't give you the right to go snooping in my personal stuff. These pictures? The trophies? This quilt? Did you ever consider that they were in that trunk for a reason? You had no right to do this. Any of this."

"Ben, I'm sorry. I didn't think—"

"No. You didn't think. You just did. You never make a plan, you just act." Ben raked a frustrated hand through his hair. "I can't deal with this right now."

He dropped the pizza on the counter as he walked back out the door.

Ben pulled out his phone, dialing as he took the elevator down to the lobby. "Hey, you busy?…Yeah, great. I'll meet you there in about ten minutes."

The air was frosty as he stepped out of his building and followed the sidewalk north. Ben jammed his phone and his hands, in the pockets of his jacket and tried to concentrate on the traffic rumbling along beside him, because if he didn't keep his mind occupied he found himself ruminating on what an ass he'd just been.

She'd just caught him by surprise. He hadn't seen a lot of that stuff for years, had kept it out of sight in that trunk because he didn't want to think about the people he'd lost. He felt enough pressure to perform, to achieve, without constant reminders of them everywhere.

Ben pulled open the door to O'Malley's Pub & Grill and stepped into the cozy restaurant with all the enthusiasm of a prisoner headed for the gallows. Calling Oz had been instinctual. Just what he always did. In the moment, it hadn't felt weird. Now, with the meeting imminent, he was acutely aware that he hadn't seen his best friend face-to-face in over a year. A couple of texts and the odd phone call. That was what twenty-five-odd years of friendship had deteriorated into.

The bar was dim, your typical brass-rails and dark-wood dive, with stained-glass dividers, beer ads lining the walls, and the requisite pool table and dartboard. There were four large-screen TVs mounted strategically throughout the room, and each and every one of them was tuned to a different sports channel.

Oz was at their usual table in the back corner. Well, it had been their usual table when they used to get together to watch Seahawks games regularly. Ben returned his wave of welcome and headed over. The waitress made eye contact with him as he was pulling off his coat, and Ben motioned toward Oz's beer. She nodded.

"How've you been, man?"

Oz stood and shook Ben's hand, punctuating it with a slap on the arm. "I was surprised you called. I thought you'd forgotten about me now that you're Mr. Hot-Shot Business Man."

"I know, and I'm sorry. Work has been crazy. I'm up for this big promotion and the hours are insane."

"Oh, yeah? Good for you."

"Haven't got it yet but it comes with a raise and a nice bonus. I was going to use it to put a down payment on the cabin."

"Are you serious?" Oz grinned. "Man, I used to love it when your dad took us to the lake to fish!"

Ben had, too. Of course, they hadn't been on the ritzy side of the lake, the one with the big rustic cabins. They'd been on the public side, casting into the water and hoping for trout. From their secret spot, they had the perfect view of this gorgeous cabin—the biggest one—across the way, and Ben's father would spin tales about how great it would be if they lived there. He spoke of silly things, like fishing from the balcony, and encouraged Ben, and Oz when he joined them, to add their own fantastical details, as well. Those were definitely some of Ben's happiest childhood memories. They'd kept up the tradition until he'd started college and been too busy to join his father.

Too busy doing things he couldn't even remember anymore. That's how unimportant they were. And now Ben would have traded almost anything to go back and make better use of the time that had run out too soon.

The waitress appeared with his Heineken, and Ben took a long swig.

"The girls miss you."

Oz's reference to his daughters brought a sad smile to Ben's face. "I miss them, too."

"Also, Jill made me promise to invite you to Amy's birthday dinner tomorrow."

"Oh, my God. She's what, five now?"

"Yeah. And a real handful."

"And? How's the team doing this year?" The flash of hurt in his friend's eyes made Ben realize he should know. A *real* friend would know.

"I like our odds for making the playoffs. I've got a good bunch of kids this round." In addition to teaching chemistry, Oz was the junior varsity men's basketball coach. "But you didn't invite me here to talk high school basketball."

"Yeah, it's… I just didn't know who else to talk to. I did something intensely stupid on that business trip in Buffalo…"

Ben hit the high points of the past week and a half, and by the time he got to Saturday night's looming dinner party, Oz was laughing at him, as he always used to do. It felt good. Like the relief of finding something you didn't even realize you were missing.

"Are you messing with me? Your bosses actually think you're married?"

"What can I say? Go big or go home, that's my motto."

"Well, as far as fuck-ups go, this one's pretty major." Oz scratched his chest. "But it's pretty cool that this girl had your back during such an epic caper, despite barely knowing you."

Ben couldn't help his smile. "Yeah. It kind of is."

"So apologize, man! Who cares if she moved some stuff. I'll bet that fancy high-rise condo of yours still looks exactly the same as it did the day I helped you unpack your couch and flat screen."

Ben scratched his eyebrow. "Not anymore. Now the wall is 'arctic mist.'"

"So you're pissed that she painted your wall?"

Ben realized how feeble that sounded. "And she opened the trunk."

"Can I be honest?"

"Sure."

"Ever since that thing with Mel, you've been different. No—" Oz cut Ben's protest off before he could make a sound. "Hear me out. Before Mel, you were easygoing, you laughed, and you never missed our weekly one-on-one game. Then she shut down your proposal and it fucked with your head. Of course it did! But you've been a different guy since then. And I'm not saying that's all bad. You're making good coin, you've got nice things, that's cool. But it sounds like this Chloe is helping to put some color back in your life, and that's great. You need that. I mean, your dad, your grandma, what good are their memories if you lock them up in a box?"

A profound question. But one that maybe Chloe could help him answer.

SHE COULDN'T SLEEP. Chloe was sitting on the couch in her pajamas, wrapped in a throw blanket, staring blankly at the TV.

She'd been in the shower when he'd come home. She'd known because his shoes were by the front door and his bedroom door was closed, even though she'd left it open earlier.

Fighting with Ben had caused a jumble of emotions to bounce around in her chest Pong-style, and she was currently veering between frustrated, anxious and sad.

She'd admitted that she'd gotten carried away. The trunk hadn't been hidden, so she hadn't thought twice about checking inside it, but she could see how Ben had found it intrusive.

She started to sigh and stopped herself, remembering the moment on the plane when Ben had noticed how often she—how had he put it?—*sighed maniacally*.

Grabbing the remote from the coffee table, Chloe flicked off the annoying infomercial for a blender. She'd made it this long without juicing anything, so why start now? Besides, she needed something stronger than juice. This situation called for the hard stuff.

She padded barefoot into the kitchen, pulled the ice cream from the freezer, and tugged off the lid, before rummaging through the drawer for a spoon. She wasn't sure if it was movement or a noise that drew her attention, but when she turned, Ben was standing in the doorway. He wore nothing but white boxer briefs, and his hair was mussed in a way that suggested some one-on-one time with his pillow. Chloe couldn't remember being more attracted to anyone in her whole life.

A warm heat throbbed to life low in her belly. Ben stepped closer, then closer still, and her hands fell limply to her sides. She didn't hear the clatter of the spoon over the thudding of her heart.

It happened in a fraction of a second, the counter suddenly boring unyieldingly into her back and Ben's mouth ravaging hers without a hint of the sweetness she'd come to expect from him. This kiss was raw, hungry, and she found herself panting in her attempts to keep up.

Chloe clawed at his shoulders, climbing his body so she could feel him between her legs. His hands left her breasts just long enough to grab her by the backs of her thighs and hoist her onto the edge of the counter. They both groaned as their bodies aligned, his cock pressing against the damp crotch of her panties, and she rocked her hips, wanting more.

He tore his mouth from hers to divest her of her Vote

Nixon T-shirt, then invaded her mouth again. Chloe whimpered. God, the man could kiss.

Then he lifted her from the counter, one arm clamped around her waist, the other raking up her spine until it was buried in her hair. Chloe ran her hands across his back, reveling in the flex of his muscles as he carried her out of the kitchen.

She kissed him with all the lust coursing through her veins, attacking his mouth with a desperation that made him stumble. With a growl, he shoved her up against the wall in the living room, and Chloe moaned as their bodies slammed together with the force that she craved. She tightened her legs around his hips and fisted her hands in his hair as he trailed his tongue behind her ear and down her neck.

Somehow they lurched their way down the hallway and into the bedroom. When they reached the bed, he set her on the mattress on her knees before joining her. Their eyes met.

Gently, he reached out and brushed the pad of his thumb across her lips. She stopped its progress with a flick of her tongue, and when Ben's eyes darkened she sucked his finger into her mouth.

With a curse Ben grabbed her, pushing her back toward the pillows. Suddenly he was on top of her, his weight a welcome burden because she craved the pressure of his erection between her thighs and his chest against her breasts.

She pushed his boxer briefs down as far as she could manage, watching unashamedly when he stood to divest himself of them. He leaned over her to kiss her stomach, yanking her panties down her thighs. Chloe thought she might orgasm from the sheer anticipation of his hot, wet kisses on her clit as they slid closer, closer...

When he pressed his mouth to her, she moaned, digging her fingers into the bed and lifting her hips, giving herself over to him. She writhed, desperate to prolong the sensation yet aching to hit the peak. The sweet pressure building in her body finally crested and broke over her in a warm rush of pleasure that stole her breath.

BEN KISSED HIS way up her body, loving the little sounds she made in the back of her throat. He nuzzled her breast, sucking her nipple into his mouth. She was so responsive, twisting with need all over again as he ran a palm over her ribs, the dip of her waist, her hip.

"Ben, I want you inside of me." Her voice was low and throaty, and he couldn't resist the pleasure of giving her what she asked for.

Her breath caught as he pushed all the way in, and she moaned, her hand on his neck, the arch of her foot stroking up and down his calf. He rocked against her, and the sweet, sliding friction of their bodies turned sharp. He drove his hips harder, spurred on by the hitch in her breath and her nails biting into his shoulders.

"Ben, please," she begged, nipping his earlobe and sending lust crashing through his body. Her hands were everywhere, his arms, his back, lower still.

She pulled him in tighter, trying to force him deeper. He knew she was close, so close, and he poured all his focus into making it good for her, into sending her over the edge.

Only after he felt her release did he let himself go, joining her in a blindingly pure orgasm.

## 12

STUPID ARCTIC MIST.

Chloe was painting again, but all her positivity from yesterday was gone, replaced with pessimism and snarls.

She'd thought the mind-blowing makeup sex had set things right between them, but when she'd woken up twenty minutes ago, it was to find that Ben had snuck out of the condo this morning without a word.

Since she couldn't leave the wall half-finished, and Saturday was fast-approaching, she'd decided to funnel her anger into manual labor. Chloe had just poured some paint into her tray when the sound of the front door startled her.

She spun to face the entrance, and very few things in the world could have shocked her more than the sight of Ben, unshaven, dressed in jeans and a white T-shirt, double fisting to-go cups from Percolate, the coffee shop down the street.

Her heart gave a little kick before she remembered she was kind of mad at him just then. "I thought you'd gone to work."

He shrugged. "I've got a day off owed to me from the

business trip. Figured I might use it today to finish off some home renos."

God, she was a sucker for stubble. She did her best to keep her stare haughty, but she could feel her anger slipping.

"You want some help?"

"Depends." Chloe shrugged noncommittally. "You have any painting experience?"

"Nope. But I have coffee, and it's been brought to my attention recently that I'm very tall."

Chloe decided conceding with grace had a certain merit. She grabbed the roller and exchanged it for the cup in his left hand. "You're hired."

Then an amazing thing happened—as they painted, he started to tell her this really great story about the cabin in the picture she loved, how he and his dad used to make up stories about it while they fished.

Chloe dipped her roller back into the paint tray, deciding whether or not she should probe the subject. Ben had gone silent at the conclusion of his story, and she didn't want to pry. Especially not after yesterday's blowup over the trunk.

But she craved knowledge about the man who stood beside her, and here, side by side, painting the living room a beautiful shade of pale gray-blue and freezing because the fumes required an open window, she was finally quenching some of that curiosity. "How come you don't have any personal stuff?" Her apartment wasn't great, but at least it was stamped with her style, her personality. "No pictures, no books, no knickknacks. I mean, it doesn't even look like you live here. How do you live your whole life without accumulating any junk?"

He glanced around the place like he was seeing it for the first time. "I never really thought about that." He ran his hand over his face, and she could hear the faint rasp of his stubble beneath his palm. "My dad wasn't very sentimental, I guess. He was more about looking to the future. I'm kind of the same way, I suppose."

"What about your mom?"

His muscles tensed. "She's the reason Dad wasn't very sentimental."

"I'm sorry."

Ben shrugged. "Not your fault."

"She wasn't around much, then?"

"Left when I was eight. Haven't heard from her since."

Chloe exhaled. "That's a really shitty thing to do to a kid."

"Yeah, well, you can't change the past, right? And my dad, he was great." Chloe could tell he'd been special, just by Ben's sad smile. "I mean, he really stepped up. Everything I have, everything I am, is because of him."

"Sounds like you were close."

He nodded.

"Can I ask what happened?"

Ben's roller stuttered on the wall, just the slightest pause and slip. When he spoke, his voice was dull. "He fell off a ladder at work."

"Oh, my God. Ben. That's awful! I'm so sorry."

"It was just a freak accident. The rung broke while he was standing on it." Ben lowered the roller, bracing the pole on the floor beside him. "He was a janitor at a big high-rise downtown. He was washing windows, something he'd done a thousand times before. And then he was just gone."

He was quiet for a long moment.

"How old were you?" she asked.

He started at the sound of her voice, as if he'd just come back from somewhere else. "I was in my second year of college, heading toward a business degree so I could get into advertising. He was really proud that I was going to make something of myself." Ben smiled, but it wobbled a bit. "That's what he always said, 'Ben, you're gonna make something of yourself.'" Ben shoved his roller into the paint and set about erasing another section of beige. "He would've liked you, though," he said without looking at her.

Chloe shook her head. The compliment was too big for her to fathom.

"He would have," Ben insisted. "He prized confidence and speaking one's mind very highly. He always told it like it was. I think you two would have really hit it off."

Now it was Chloe's turn to be silent. She needed a minute to take that in.

"I'm sorry I went into that trunk without your permission, Ben."

He shrugged. "I was just surprised. I haven't seen that stuff in quite a while. I wasn't prepared."

Chloe understood that now. But she wanted to explain. "It felt like a treasure chest, you know? I mean, I thought it was so cool that you had all this stuff, all these reminders of the people you love and the people who loved you. I never considered for a moment that you wouldn't want those memories."

She'd finished the lower part of the wall, and she figured Ben would be done in a few more strokes of the roller. She stepped back to take in their handiwork.

"You must have the same."

"No, actually," she confessed, and Ben glanced over his shoulder at her.

"I don't have those kind of memories with my dad. He was always working. Still is. Sometimes I realize that I barely know him. I definitely don't have any pictures like these." She ran a hand across the top of the frame that held the shot of the Masterson men fishing. "All of our family photos are stiff and formal and taken by very expensive photographers."

Ben lowered his roller from the finished wall. "Different worlds, huh?"

"Completely."

They both turned their attention to the wall. It looked even better than she'd imagined, but her current feeling of satisfaction had nothing to do with arctic mist. "Pretty good, huh?"

Ben nodded. "It's growing on me. Chloe?"

"Yeah?"

"Are you busy tonight?"

"No."

"How would you like to go to a birthday party with me?"

"You sure you're okay?" Ben was staring at her with concern, the apple pie he'd picked up at the amazing bakery near their place—his place, she corrected herself—balanced on one hand as they made their way up the sidewalk to Oz's house.

"I'm great," she lied, motioning toward the jacked-up red Toyota Tundra parked at the curb. "I'm still hung up on the fact that's your vehicle, Masterson. A Lexus? Yes. A Beamer? Sure. But a pick-up? I wouldn't have guessed that in a million years."

Ben glanced back at it. "What's wrong with my truck?"

"The truck is fine. You seem a little too city to be driving it, that's all."

He scoffed at her summation, and she returned his eyeroll as she ran her hands down her stomach ostensibly smoothing a wrinkle in her coat. In truth, she was trying to calm the raging herd of butterflies in combat boots that had taken over her stomach.

Meeting the friends. It felt like a big deal. It *was* a big deal.

She'd agreed in a moment of extreme weakness. He'd just told her about his father, they'd had a nice day painting, and she'd been blinded by the intimacy of it all.

*A party? Sure, I'll go to a party with you.*

By the time she'd found out it was a party for a five-year-old and they'd be the only adults there save for his oldest and dearest friend and his wife, she'd been trapped.

She glanced down at her left hand—at Ben's grandmother's wedding ring, for God's sake!—its symbolic weight tethering her to a man she had nothing in common with.

They ascended the front steps and before she knew it, Ben was knocking on the door. Chloe took a deep breath and pulled the ring off her left hand, transferring it to her right. An attempt to keep a little perspective before she went down the rabbit hole.

The door opened to reveal a lovely, fresh-faced redhead with the harried look of a mother—a look that said she'd just handled about twenty things before appearing before them. Her slightly frizzy curls were scraped back from her face in a ponytail, and she wore jeans, slippers and a purple sweatshirt with a big, gold W on the front. Obviously a proud University of Washington alum. Her face lit up when she recognized her guests—well, one of them—and she pushed open the screen.

"We brought grown-up dessert." Ben raised the pie as proof.

"You are a saint, Ben." She relieved him of his delicious burden. "You know how much I hate confetti cupcakes. How come I didn't marry you instead of Oz?"

"I'm pretty sure it's because I didn't ask you."

"Right. How gallant of you to remind me. And why was that again?"

"Couldn't do it. My best friend was in love with you, and you remember the rule, Jilly: bros before hos."

The woman's laughter was full-bodied and infectious; Chloe liked her immediately.

"Well, if that's the case then we hos need to stick together. You must be Chloe. I'm Jill, Seth's wife. Please come in. And watch out for beads. There was a necklace-making catastrophe earlier, and they keep rolling out of nowhere and attacking people's feet, no matter how much I vacuum." She shut the door behind them. "I guess I should be thankful it was beads. The last calamity involved an ant farm."

"Uncle Ben! You're here!"

Two of the cutest children Chloe had ever seen raced in out of nowhere, and Jill used the distraction to disappear into the kitchen with the pie.

"There they are! How're my girls?" Ben reached down to scoop the youngest into his arm. Her bright red curls, just like her mom's, glowed around a face full of freckles. The older girl had tucked herself against Ben's leg, and his hand rested protectively against her shoulder. Her brown hair was also curly, but the ringlets were far more subdued than her sister's—just like her personality.

"We missed you!"

"Aw, I missed you guys, too. Chloe, meet Laura and Ragamuffin."

The girl in his arms giggled. "Uncle Beh-en. My *name* is *Amy.*"

"Oh, right. *Amy*. I keep forgetting that!"

Chloe couldn't help but smile. "It's nice to meet you, Amy. I'm Chloe."

"I'm five today," Amy announced, holding up the requisite number of fingers.

"That's right! I heard there was a birthday girl in the house," Ben said. He looked down as Laura tugged on his pants.

"Uncle Ben," Laura whispered, her green eyes large as she motioned for him to bend down. Cupping her hand to his ear, she leaned close to impart her secret.

Ben's resulting smile tugged at Chloe's heart. "So do I. Why don't you tell her so? I think she'd be happy to hear that."

Shyly, Laura turned to Chloe. "I like your hair."

Startled, Chloe's gaze bounced from Laura's to Ben's, then back to Laura's. "Oh. Thanks." She recovered with a smile. "I… I like yours, too. I always wanted curly hair." The little girl smiled, revealing that the tooth fairy must have visited her recently, before she hid her face against Ben's coat.

"All right, who wants to try to defeat me at Candyland?" he said.

"I do, I do!" and "Me, me, me!" got all jumbled up as Laura and Amy vied for his attention. He bent down and set Amy on the linoleum.

"Okay, you ladies go get the game set up and I will be in after I say hi to your mom and dad. Deal?"

"Deal!" they shouted, scampering off toward the living room. Ben reached into the front closet and grabbed a hanger, motioning for Chloe to hand him her coat, which she did.

"Smells good," he called to Jill as he hung up her

coat, then divested himself of his own and gave it the same treatment.

"Oz not back yet?"

"He texted after the game ended. I'm expecting him in about ten minutes."

"Cool. Did you need any help?"

Jill shook her head. "I've got things under control. But thanks."

"Then if you'll excuse me, I have a Candyland grudge-match to attend to. Winner takes all. Coming?" Ben asked her, and his smile was so inviting that Chloe thought she might follow him anywhere.

"Forget it." Jill jumped in. "I need news of the outside world! No way am I letting you steal away my adult company. Chloe's staying in the kitchen with me."

"Okay, but don't let her start on the pie." Chloe made a face but he'd already headed into the other room.

"Ben's really great with your girls."

Jill smiled and led Chloe deeper into the kitchen. "Yeah, they love him. You can put your purse here," she offered as they passed a small table littered with spelling tests and mail. "But enough about Ben. I love my kids and all, but I can't tell you how excited I am by the prospect of a little adult conversation with someone who doesn't have children. Are bars still as fun as I remember? What's it like not to have to schedule sex? In my foggy memories, it seemed hot, but my practical mom brain is having a hard time with the logistics of shaving. I mean, do you have to do it every day? Just in case? Because I'm not sure if that's worth it."

Chloe laughed, settling onto one of the stools at the breakfast bar.

Jill stood on the opposite side of the kitchen island, ripping into a bag of croutons and sprinkling them onto a Caesar salad. "Watch out for plum sauce before you touch the counter. The girls had chicken fingers earlier."

Dutifully, Chloe ran a hand over the Formica in front of her and, deeming it safe, rested her sweater-covered elbow on it. "The girls already ate? I thought this was Amy's birthday party."

"Today is her birthday, but she's not having friends over until Saturday. To be honest, Oz just wanted to meet you, but he's a big chicken, so instead of inviting you over, he used Amy's birthday as an excuse. He's been like that since the seventh grade."

"You met your husband in middle school?"

Jill nodded. "Sure did. Ben, too. Seth and I started dating when I turned fifteen, and that is the end of that very short story. But it's how I know that you might just be the first thing Ben's ever kept secret from Oz. That worries him. It means you're different."

The sudden panic burrowing in her gut must have showed on her face because Jill laughed.

"That was a no-pressure statement," Jill assured her, pulling on some oven mitts that looked like frogs. "I heard you two haven't known each other long. To be honest, I'm just glad I got the chance to meet you." She reached into the oven and turned the lasagna around before placing a couple of foil-covered bags of garlic bread on the rack beside it.

"Ben hasn't been around much lately, but even when he came consistently, he was never one to bring a lady friend. Said he didn't want to subject my girls to the instability. How adorable is that?" she asked, closing the door and pulling the heat-resistant amphibians off her hands. "He hasn't come to the house with a woman in ages—not since the engagement was called off."

Chloe's head snapped up. "Ben was engaged?" Her

body tingled and a wave of numbness washed over her, like she'd been dosed with a shot of Novocain.

Jill bit her lip. "Crap. He didn't tell you. I just thought, because of the ring…"

Chloe shook her head, hating that she glanced at her left hand first. When she looked up again, Jill seemed to be in the midst of an internal battle. Her shoulders sagged as she made her decision.

"Okay, you didn't hear this from me, but now that I've let the cat out of the bag… Her name was Melanie. She's a lawyer. Nice enough—a little uppity, but she tried. I don't think a high school chemistry teacher and a dental hygienist were quite impressive enough for her taste, but Ben seemed to like her, so I gave her a chance. Then she left Ben for some old guy with a lot of money. Ben's been knocking himself out climbing the corporate ladder ever since."

"I, uh. Wow."

Jill nodded. "Pretty pivotal moment, I guess. And I'm sure it's the main reason Seth is so intent on checking you out for himself."

The sudden sound of a door banging open stole their attention. "Is that lasagna I smell?"

Jill smiled brightly. "Speak of the devil. Welcome home, hon. How was the tournament?"

"Not bad. Came in third. I'll fill you in after, since I saw Ben's truck out front. Oh, hey."

Oz stepped into the kitchen. He was nothing like she'd imagined. Decent-looking, but he was a bit baby-faced and in the beginning stages of male-pattern baldness. Not the fit, cocky executive type she'd been expecting of Ben's best friend. Just a normal guy.

"Chloe, right?"

She nodded.

"Interesting hair."

Jill's head snapped around and she glared at her husband.

Still, Chloe smiled sweetly, despite the implied insult. "Thanks. Oz, right?"

He nodded, a little warily if she wasn't mistaken.

"Interesting name. Your mom spent some time in the back of the Black Sabbath tour bus? Dad was a closet Judy Garland fan?"

She was prepared for eye daggers, but instead Oz broke into hearty laughter. "It's Seth Osbourne, actually, but I like the way you handled that. Test passed. Where have you been all Ben's life?"

"What?"

"I'm gonna be straight with you, Chloe, because I know my wife has already told you about Melanie." He sent Jill a sidelong glance, but she kept her gaze focused on the utensil drawer as she counted out forks and knives. "Ben and I have been friends since the third grade, and I've never seen someone mess with his head the way Melanie did. Then he says that he's fake married to some woman he met on a plane, and I feel the need to vet her. But I understand why he likes you. So, unless there comes a time when I have to take sides between you, we're cool."

Now it was Chloe's turn to laugh. He might not look like he and Ben ran in the same circles, but Chloe no longer had any doubts that they were soul mates. "All right then. I accept your terms."

"Great. How much longer until dinner?"

Jill glanced at the oven timer. "Fifteen minutes."

"See you then. If I know my girls, I've got a Candyland game to win." Oz headed for the living room.

"It's time for pjs!" she called after him, and he saluted

her without breaking stride. Jill shot Chloe a droll look. "So you can appreciate why I had to lock that down back in high school. Can you even imagine the bidding war if he was still single?"

"GOT ROOM FOR one more?"

Ben glanced up as Oz sauntered into the room in his usual coaching uniform—khakis and a school-logoed polo shirt.

"Daddy, you can be on my team!" Laura's invitation came with a hug as she hopped up and ran over to greet Oz.

"All right, pumpkin. But first, Mommy wants you two to get into your pajamas. Then you can come back down and we'll finish the game and have cupcakes, okay?"

"But Daddy, I'm winning!" Laura protested.

"And you'll still be winning when you're in your pajamas," Oz assured her, reaching out a hand to help Amy out of Ben's lap. "Up we go, Carrot-Girl." He gave each of his girls a kiss and shooed them up the stairs.

Silence settled in their absence, and Oz scraped a hand through his hair with a loud exhale before grabbing a seat.

"So I met your lady."

"She's not so much my lady as my fake wife."

Oz shot him an unimpressed look. "Whatever, Benny. I saw the ring. Fool yourself if you must, but don't try to fool me."

"What's that supposed to mean?" The problem with friends you'd known your whole life was that they'd known you just as long. And they weren't shy about pointing out things you weren't quite ready to admit.

"It means that your grandma's ring isn't something that you give away lightly. I seem to remember four agonizing months of back-and-forth on whether you were even willing to give it to the woman you asked to marry you for real. You're like Gollum with that ring, always have been. So the fact you handed it over to Chloe after a day? That means something. Don't act as if it doesn't."

"Whatever, man. I told you. We got caught post-coital by a client and I panicked and said we were married to save face. We needed a ring fast so we could make it to breakfast on time."

"Bullshit, moneybags. You probably had a bunch of options. Hotel jewelry store, she coulda borrowed something from one of her relatives. Hell, I'll bet you didn't even ask Chloe if she had something that could pass before you had that ring on her finger."

Ben snapped his mouth shut, hoping the color crawling up his neck wasn't as red as it felt. That wasn't how it had gone down. Not exactly. He liked Chloe, sure, but he wasn't…they weren't…

"Your dad woulda liked her," Oz said softly.

Hearing Oz echo the words he'd said earlier sucked the oxygen out of his lungs.

"And more importantly, so do I." Oz bowed his head. "You may proceed."

The jab of humor let the air back in the room, and Ben reached for it like a life preserver. "I appreciate that, since your approval means everything to me."

"I'm glad because I would be happy to dole out more approval if you'll come out to the garage and help me change out my broken taillight. I'm hoping your delicate fingers will have better luck where my manly hands have failed."

"Sure…right after I kick your ass at Candyland."

"Oh, them's fightin' words, Benny-boy." Oz got off his chair and joined Ben beside the game board on the carpet. "Hand me that green gingerbread man."

# 13

CHLOE YAWNED AS she padded into the kitchen the next morning. She'd had a shower, changed out of her pajamas and brushed her teeth, but despite all that, she was pretty sure her eyes were still half-closed. Luckily her other senses had kicked into high gear and the scent of coffee proved enough to guide her to the safety of the mug cupboard.

Ben, who seemed to have none of the cognitive dissonance associated with being awake at five-thirty in the morning—Was it night? Was it day? Chloe's body couldn't decide—was lounging at the kitchen table, sipping coffee, reading something on his tablet and looking perfectly wide-awake. Damn his handsome, handsome face.

"Remind me why you're up at 5:30 a.m. again?" she asked.

"I've got a lunch meeting today, so I'm going to hit the gym before work."

"That is the grossest thing I've ever heard. At least I *have* to be at the store at six. I'll be fired if I'm not there to let the plumber in to fix the leak."

Chloe set her coffee on the table, and took the seat next

to him at the small, square dining table. He looked up from his tablet.

"Yeah, well I…" he trailed off, staring at her with a really weird expression on his face.

"Well you…?" she prodded.

"I, uh…"

Chloe frowned at him. "What is up with you?"

"I've never seen you without makeup before."

Her hand flew to her cheek. *Oh, God.* She never forgot her makeup. Not even at this ungodly time of the morning.

"You look different."

"Different bad?" she guessed, wishing he'd stop staring so intently. Chloe felt more vulnerable in that moment than if she'd been sitting there completely nude with an audience watching them.

"No. Just different. Softer. I like it." Ben reached over and dragged his thumb across her bare lips. Then he leaned forward and pressed his lips to hers in the softest, most sensual kiss she'd ever experienced. He thanked her when he pulled away.

"For what?" she asked as he got up from the table and put his coffee mug in the sink.

"For finally trusting me with the real you."

"What? No. What?" That was not what this was. It had been a judgement lapse, the mistake of a sleep-deprived mind! An anomaly.

He kissed the top of her head and grabbed the duffle bag he'd left beside the door. "See you later, Chloe. Have a good day at work."

*What the hell had just happened?*

She made herself stay calmly seated at the table until Ben had left for the gym, but the split second the door closed behind him she made a run for her makeup case.

THE PLUMBER WAS done long before Titanium Beauty was set to open, but instead of heading home, Chloe treated herself to breakfast before her shift and made a list of supplies she'd need for the looming dinner party. An earlier inventory of Ben's cupboards showed he was woefully understocked in most of the necessities, from place mats to aperitifs to a decent cheese board.

Luckily, after work she managed to pick up the basics at decent prices. Thank God for big box stores.

Once she'd unpacked, washed and put everything where she could find it tomorrow, Chloe found herself at a bit of a loss. She'd prepped everything, the house was clean, and Ben probably wouldn't be home until late.

She decided on some cereal for dinner, and afterward Chloe settled onto the couch with a blanket and a bag of microwave popcorn, excited to take full advantage of the fact that she had the place to herself for a couple of hours and Ben had a Netflix subscription.

She was scrolling through "Top Picks for Ben"—she was dying to know what he'd watched to get both *Breaking Bad* and *Downton Abbey* to show up in his list—when her mother's special ringtone broke the silence.

There had been a pretty sizable spike in the frequency of her mother's calls since she'd found out that her eldest daughter had managed to snag herself a man. And though it bothered her if she thought about how infrequent the calls had been before her fake engagement, she had to admit that talking to her mother wasn't as bad as she used to think. In fact, it was kind of nice having her mom check in with her life once in a while.

"Hello?"

"Chloe, it's your mom."

"Hey, Mom. What's up?"

"We're downstairs."

"I'm sorry, what?"

"We're in the lobby of your building, but we don't know what button to push for the buzzer. There aren't any names, and none of the numbers match yours. Yes, Daryl. I told her there aren't any names."

Chloe shook her head, trying to clear it. "You're in Seattle? Right now?"

"Daryl, don't just hit random buttons!"

*Yep. This was happening.*

"Mom? Mom, don't push any more buttons," Chloe implored, getting up from the couch. "I'm buzzing you in, okay?" Chloe hurried into the kitchen and hit the number on Ben's landline that would allow them access. "Come up to the third floor. Apartment 325."

Chloe hung up both phones and set them on the counter. *Unbelievable.*

She went through all the stages of shock before she heard her parents chattering in the hallway. She pulled open the door before they had a chance to knock.

"What are you guys doing here? When you asked for the address the other day, I thought it was because you were sending something. In the mail."

"Well, I was going to. But since Caroline and Dalton are still on their honeymoon, and we knew that *you* wouldn't be flying back to Buffalo to visit any time *soon*, we figured why not stop by for a visit and hand deliver our present on our way to Hawaii."

Chloe forced a smile.

"We called the travel agent and had her change our tickets so we had an extra long layover in Seattle, and here we are!"

"Here you are!" Chloe repeated. She looked around. "Where's your stuff?"

"Oh, we left it back at our hotel. We're staying at the Four Seasons."

Chloe sagged with relief. *Thank God.*

"Except for this!" Her mom grabbed the large gift-wrapped rectangle from her father's grasp and shoved it into Chloe's hands. "Are you surprised?"

"I really am," she said, meaning the words on so many levels.

Her father cleared his throat. "Are you going to invite us in?"

"Yes, of course! Sorry, Dad." Chloe stepped out of the way so her parents could enter. "You can just throw your coats on the bench there."

Chloe turned and brought her present—a picture frame, there was no doubt in her mind—over to the coffee table, leaving her parents to trail in her wake.

"Where's Benjamin hiding?"

"He's still at work."

"Good man. What time will he be home?"

"I'm not sure, Dad."

"Well, that's a shame. Your father and I were so looking forward to seeing him, weren't we, Daryl?"

"Where's the remote?"

Her mother perched herself on the arm of the couch, her eyes darting around the room. "What a lovely apartment this is, Chloe! The colors are exquisite, and it feels so homey. Who's your decorator?"

Something disconcertingly like pride bloomed in Chloe's chest as she handed her dad the remote, even though part of her brain was chastising her for it. "Actually, Ben and I did it ourselves."

"Well, it looks amazing. And it goes perfectly with your gift. Why don't you open it and see?"

Chloe had expected the frame, but the three black-and-white photos mounted inside it blindsided her. The top photo captured Ben twirling her on the dance floor. The bottom photo was taken from behind, showing her and Ben holding hands as they left the reception. Her favorite, though, was the middle one, where she was laughing and Ben was grinning at her.

Despite their fancy clothes and the glitz and glam behind them, they looked genuine. And happy. The memory of that moment—when "Sweet Caroline" had filled the room—made her smile.

"Do you like it?"

"Mom, it's amazing. Really. I love it. Thank you so much. I can't wait to hang it."

The jingle of keys sounded, and she looked up as Ben pushed through the door.

"Ben! I wasn't expecting you home yet. You remember my parents?"

He froze, but quickly recovered and flashed that smile of his. "Of course. Fiona, Daryl. Good to see you again."

Her mother beamed.

"You'll have to excuse me. I just got off work. Let me get cleaned up and I'll be right out."

"You take all the time you need, Benjamin. Don't hurry on our account."

Chloe frowned. *Don't hurry on our account?* Who was this person, and what had she done with Fiona Masterson?

"We're just thrilled to spend some time visiting with our daughter and her fiancé."

Confusion rumpled Ben's brow, and she remembered that she'd lied to him about explaining the true situation to her parents. She begged him wordlessly to play along. "Oh, yeah, right. Us, too. Chloe, can I talk to you for a second?" His voice was a little too level, and it raised the hair on the back of her neck.

"Of course, sweetie!" *Crap, crap, crap.* She followed him to the bedroom, but when he pulled the door closed and spun around to face her, she cut him off before he could open his mouth.

"Ben, I lied to you at the gift opening. I didn't set them straight. I let them believe we're engaged. I'm sorry. I don't know why I didn't tell them the truth." Chloe wrung her hands, and the bite of her fake engagement ring pricked her conscience.

"Okay, yes, I do know why. I let them believe it because it made them happy. And I didn't expect them to visit! They never visit! But they really like your apartment, and they really like the way the living room is decorated, and my mother's been here for six minutes already and has only mentioned Caroline *once*, which is unheard of, and I just… I just wanted to hold onto that feeling, okay? But I'll tell them the truth. I'll go out there right now if you want me to and say that I lied to them, that we were never engaged. If that's what you want me to do, I'll do it."

Chloe looked at Ben expectantly, willing him to understand, to help her out. His slightly dazed expression began to clear as he processed the situation. He opened his mouth to speak. "I—"

"*Please* don't make me go back out there and break the truth to them! I am *begging* you. They're staying at the Four Seasons tonight and they're off to Hawaii tomorrow. You just have to pretend we're engaged for one evening. A couple of well-timed endearments, a few half truths, and a peck on the cheek, that's all I'm asking! I will owe you so big for this. Huge! Ask, and it shall be done."

"You want me to pretend I'm your fiancé?"

"Yes, Masterson. Keep up with me here. We don't have much time before our being in the bedroom is going to start looking suspicious."

"Trust me, the irony is not lost on me that I'm the one who's asking, but are you sure you want to do this?"

Chloe was dumbfounded. "Why wouldn't I be sure? Aren't we already doing it?"

"Chloe, this is your family."

"So?"

"So that makes it different. Different than lying to a business acquaintance. Different than lying to your boss. It has to be."

His naïveté was adorable.

"Ben, do you know the last time my parents visited me in the four years since I moved to Seattle?"

He shook his head.

"Never, Ben. They have *never* been here to see me before. This is their fourth trip to Hawaii during the same time frame. The only reason they came now is because I'm finally engaged. To a great guy, with a great job."

He exhaled on a sigh. "Fine. If you're sure this is what you want to do." Ben pulled his suit jacket off and loosened his tie. "Give me fifteen minutes for a shower and I'll be right out."

Chloe couldn't hold back a smile, relief tingling through her chest. "Thank you, Ben. I really appreciate it. "

"AND PRESTO! I'VE FINALLY made them disappear," she joked a few hours later.

"I know they drive you crazy, but you were great tonight."

She laughed. "No, *you* were great. I was just the unfortunate by-product they had to endure in order to bask in your awesomeness. But truthfully, that was the best evening I've ever spent with them."

And that wasn't hyperbole, either.

Ben gave her one of those long, hard looks that took the shine off her mood. "You realize you're going to have to tell them the truth eventually, right?"

"Yes." Chloe nodded, suddenly realizing that after tomorrow's business dinner ended, so did pleasant evenings with her parents and sexy, sultry nights with Ben. Had it really only been a week and a half since they'd met?

"Speaking of which, what's your own plan for that?" she asked. "The confessing? I mean, you're going to need to come clean with your bosses someday."

A slight frown marred his forehead as he loaded their wineglasses into the dishwasher and pushed the door closed. "Yeah, I guess I will. I hadn't really put too much thought into that half of the operation. I'll play the divorce card, I suppose."

It was a weird topic of conversation, so Chloe wasn't completely shocked when an awkward silence reared its head.

Ben broke first. "I've got some work I still need to get done tonight. I'll be in my office. I'll try not to wake you when I come to bed."

He smiled at her, gave her a kiss on the cheek and left the living room.

"Okay, yeah. Sure. Don't stay up too late," she said.

And just like that, Chloe knew.

The cleaning, the prepping, the not wearing makeup. How many times had she seen her mother do the same thing?

With a flash of certainty that made her knees weak, Chloe admitted the painfully obvious.

She was in love with Ben.

# 14

"WHAT IS UP with you today?" Josh asked.

"Nothing. I'm fine."

Love was making her crabby, but she certainly wasn't going to tell Josh that. She'd filled him in on the real story behind Ben in a moment of weakness during their last shift and he hadn't shut up about it.

"Bull crap. You've got a serious case of bitch-face today and you'd better do something about it because you're scaring the customers. I've helped three women in the last half hour who were headed your way until they caught sight of your sour expression. I say this as your friend and your employee: you're the manager of a store in the service industry. You're contractually obligated to smile."

Chloe pasted on a fake grin and batted her eyelashes at him. "Better?"

A woman stepped up beside her. "Excuse me, do you work here?"

"She sure does." Josh backed away with a smug little wave of his fingers, and Chloe readjusted her grimace into a more natural-looking smile as she turned to face the woman.

"What can I help you with?"

The blonde smiled. "Well, I'm getting married on Valentine's Day."

"Oh, congratulations!" Chloe tried to sound excited, because she knew it was expected, but her fake marriage was such a huge pain in the ass right now she found herself pretty tepid on the whole wedding issue.

"Thanks. But I was just walking by and I realized I haven't thought much about wedding makeup yet. I just love how you did your eyes. They look incredible."

"Thank you." Chloe smiled, genuinely this time. Nothing like a makeup compliment to douse the bitterness of falling in real love with your fake husband.

The woman hitched her purse higher on her shoulder. "Do you think you could get the same effect if you used lighter colors?" she asked.

"Yes, you could definitely create a more subtle version of this look. Were you planning on wearing peach shades? Because with your skin tone, I would recommend something like this—" she plucked an eye shadow pot from the display "—with this color on the lid and this color in the crease." Chloe placed the shadows she'd selected in the woman's hands. "Add a golden highlight and a strong brow, and your eyes will look incredible. Oh, and we've got this great waterproof mascara, too. A definite must for the big day."

Forty minutes later, Chloe had walked the woman—Joanna, she discovered—through foundation, lips and cheeks, and was handing over a silver Titanium Beauty bag full of all the cosmetics and brushes the other woman would need for her wedding day.

"There you go. Play with it a little and try some of the techniques we talked about. If you have any questions, feel free to call the store."

"Thanks, Chloe. I'm terrified I'm not going to come close to what you've described. I don't suppose you do offsite makeup applications?"

"Sure, I could do that." The words slipped off her tongue without conscious thought, and the store manager part of her brain was screaming in protest. She was supposed to say, "I'm afraid all our makeup services are only offered in-store," but Ben's voice sounded in her head.

*Makeup by Chloe could be whatever you want it to be.* His voice had been popping into her mind a lot lately.

"Really? That would be amazing. How can I book you?"

Chloe took a deep breath and committed to putting herself out there. "Let's book it right now. I'm free on Valentine's Day, you just tell me where to be and when. But in the interest of full disclosure, I should tell you that I'll be doing your makeup as an independent makeup artist, not as an employee of Titanium Beauty."

Joanna smiled. "That's fine, as long as you say you can do the bridesmaids' makeup too."

Moments later, Chloe walked back to the counter, her phone number programmed into Joanna's phone, and a trial makeup appointment scheduled for the following weekend.

"Did you just do what I think you just did, Miz Store Manager?"

"Hmm?" She cocked her head toward the sound of Josh's voice, but she was distracted. She'd done it! She'd taken the first step toward turning Makeup by Chloe into something more than a far-off dream. And it was pretty damn empowering.

Not that she had much of a choice. After tonight's dinner, things were going to change, and she was not going to let her suddenly charmed life turn back into a pumpkin without a fight.

"Look at you go! One minute you're pouting over the eye shadow display and the next you're making sales and breaking rules."

"I didn't—"

"Yes, you did. You know damn well you just conflict-of-interest-ed all over that situation. And I love it! You are way too talented to be spending your days worrying about the break schedule. I think it's great that you're claiming your rightful place as Queen of the Makeup Jungle."

Chloe laughed, secretly pleased by Josh's enthusiasm. "You're in a good mood. What's gotten into you?"

He pursed his lips and raised an eyebrow. "I think the question is what's gotten into *you*. And I'm pretty sure the answer is Businessman Ben's penis."

"*Ugh*. Josh. This is exactly why I don't tell you anything."

"Chad and I were discussing it, and—"

"You and your boyfriend were discussing Ben's junk? You've met him once, and Chad's never laid eyes on him."

"I may have snapped a covert photo of him when he came in here to sweep you into this hot, sexy lie you've been living for the past week. But that's beside the point. He's shaken up your status quo. Before him, you would never have put yourself out there like that. Don't argue." He held up a hand, and she closed her mouth.

"I hope this appointment proves to you that you can be an awesome businesswoman. Because I will quit this job in an instant to come work for you when you get Makeup by Chloe off the ground. At least until the band hits it big."

"Josh, that was almost a really sweet thing to say. And since you brought up the band, I was wondering…"

"Yeah?"

"Would you guys be interested in writing a riff that I could use at the beginning of my YouTube videos? I'm thinking of upgrading my production value."

"I'M SURE THERE'S A 'Honey, I'm home' joke in this somewhere, but it feels way too obvious," Chloe announced, pushing through the apartment door with a garment bag and a shoe box. She'd swung by her apartment on the way home from work to pick up a couple of things—namely her favorite black Alexander McQueen dress, her studded Valentino pumps and the pearls she'd received for her sixteenth birthday.

They were the only remnants of her old life that she'd kept, because regardless of their designer labels, they made her feel strong and powerful. And because being ready and appropriate for any occasion was a virtue that her mother had drilled into her from an early age. And if they were going to pull off this business dinner, convince people who knew Ben well that they were a couple, she was going to need all the help she could get.

"Oh, my *God*! What is that amazing smell?"

"Ben Masterson's Famous Mediterranean Chicken." He glanced over his shoulder at her but there was panic in his eyes. She'd never seen Ben so nervous. She wished he'd taken her suggestion and gotten this shindig catered instead of cooking dinner himself. He was under enough pressure.

"Everything in control?"

"I think so. Salad's in the fridge, chicken's in the oven. What's in the bags?"

"Just my outfit for tonight." She turned toward the closet, tucking the shoe box on the floor and hanging the garment bag on the far right side.

He joined her in the foyer.

"You look happy."

She nodded as he stepped toward her, wrapping his arms around her waist and pulling her close.

She put her hands around his neck. "I had a really good day today."

"Oh, yeah?"

Again, she nodded, pulling his mouth to hers. He looked a little woozy by the time she finally broke the kiss.

"Got a few minutes?"

He glanced over his shoulder at the kitchen. "I think so. What did you have in mind?"

"Well, like I said…" Chloe hooked her fingers in the front of his belt and began tugging him toward the bedroom. "I had a really good day." She wanted to tell him everything, how she'd finally worked up the courage to take a chance on her dream business. She'd even priced out a couple of laptops when her shift was over. And it was all because of him. All those possibilities he'd painted the other night? She could see them now.

But tonight Ben had other things on his mind, and rightfully so. Tonight it was *his* dream on the line. But at the very least, she could help him relax a little.

She pulled him through the apartment and didn't stop until they reached the foot of the bed. Her fingers made quick work of his belt buckle. She undid the button on his jeans, and pulled his zipper down slowly.

"And now I want to make sure that you're having a good day, too. How does that sound?" Maintaining eye contact, she lowered herself to her knees in front of him.

"That sounds incredible," he managed to answer. His eyes never left hers, and Chloe loved the intensity of his gaze as she drove him to the edge. She dragged his jeans down his thighs, revealing his straining muscles and white boxer-briefs. "Is this for me?" she asked, running her finger along the length of his very impressive bulge, and Ben made a strangled sound in his throat.

He had such a beautiful body, and she wanted to see more of it. "Take off your shirt."

He obliged, shedding his white T-shirt in a matter of seconds. His entire torso was so damn incredible; she couldn't help but lean forward and press a kiss to his stomach, and his hips jerked in frustration.

"You're killing me, Chloe." His voice was strained, rough, and she loved that he loved what she was doing to him. It turned her on.

She took pity on him, divesting him of his underwear so that he stood naked and proud. With a Cheshire smile, she leaned forward and ran her tongue along the length of his shaft. His groan of pleasure made her stomach clench.

"More. Please. Don't stop."

She held the base of his cock, her lips engulfing the tip, pausing for a moment before she took as much of him as she could handle into her mouth. She sucked her way back up to the top before lowering her head again, this time taking him so deep her lips touched her hand.

"That feels amazing." Ben curled one big hand into her hair, but he let her set the rhythm. She read the reactions of his body, speeding up and slowing down in response to his groans and the slight undulation of his hips.

"Chloe, I'm— I can't hold back much longer."

She engulfed the length of him one final time, working her way back to the tip slowly and with more pressure. His hand tightened in her hair. She released his cock, staring up at him to find his head back and his eyes closed, his muscles straining. With a satisfied smile, Chloe got to her feet.

"Did you like that?" she asked, because she needed to hear him say it.

He opened his eyes, let go of her hair and put his hand to her cheek. "It was amazing." He caught her mouth in a rough kiss that reminded her that she wasn't nearly done with him.

"Well, there's more where that came from," she promised. "Just lie back and let me do all the work."

"How can I say no to that?" He climbed onto the mattress and lay against the pillows. She could feel his eyes on her as she peeled off her clothes, dropping them piece by piece.

She crawled onto the mattress and inched toward him, planting one hand on his chest and squeezing his hips between her thighs as she straddled him. Then she reached between them and guided him inside her, right where she ached to feel him most. She loved the way he filled her. And then, staring into his eyes, she began to move.

*Hell, yes.* THERE WEREN'T enough curse words to accurately express just how blown his mind was at this point. Chloe had driven him wild with her mouth, and now, watching her use him for her own pleasure, feeling her tight, slick heat consuming him, well, he could get used to this kind of torture.

He loved the way her breath caught in her throat when she rubbed against him just the right way. Hell, he loved it all; the bounce of her breasts, the undulation of her body as she rode him, it was so damn erotic.

"Chloe, tell me how good it feels for you."

"So good," she breathed. She planted both hands on his chest and began rocking back and forth, and the change in pace swamped him with unexpected pleasure.

He drove his hips upward, trying to get higher, deeper inside her, and she shuddered.

"Oh, my God, Ben. Do that again," she begged, and he was powerless to disobey. Grabbing her by the hips, he pressed his thumbs into the bird tattoos at her hips and drove himself high inside her once, twice. Then she cried out, her muscles contracting around him, and he let himself drown in a sweet, hot wave of ecstasy.

CHLOE SNUGGLED CLOSER to his big body, deliciously spent, and was just nodding off when the screech of the smoke detector startled them both out of their dreamy haze.

"Oh, shit! The chicken!"

Ben was out of bed and into his boxers so fast that Chloe barely had enough time to register what was happening. She pulled on his discarded T-shirt and rushed toward the kitchen, only to be greeted with a smoky haze.

"Get the door," he ordered, and she rushed over to pull open the sliding glass door of the balcony so Ben, clad in boxers and oven mitts, could take the charred, smoldering mess outside and place it on the patio table.

He stormed back into the condo, disappearing around the corner into the hallway, and a moment later, the shrill beeping of the smoke detector went silent.

Chloe opened the window in the dining area as well to help clear the smoke.

"What the hell am I going to do now? They're going to be here in," he glanced at the clock on the wall and then turned a ghostly shade of pale, "forty minutes! I can't believe this happened. I was supposed to reduce the heat for the last hour. You shouldn't have distracted me."

"You weren't complaining a minute ago," she reminded him archly.

"I don't have time for jokes right now. I need this dinner to go well. I need this promotion," he reminded her. "This is my whole life on the line!"

"It's not your whole life. It's only money."

"Easy for you to say. You grew up with enough of it."

"Ben, come on. This doesn't matter that much! Don't you see that? They don't care about you or the damn burnt chicken! It's a game, Ben, just like when Burke showed up for breakfast. You should realize that, but you're too blinded by this never-ending quest for power and status! Do you think that's really what your father wanted for you? "

"You're going to lecture me about success?" Ben raked a hand through his hair. "You're telling me you dropped out of law school to sell makeup at the mall? I don't buy it, Chloe! You're sitting on your dream job but you're too damn scared to pull the trigger!"

"This isn't about me, Ben. It's about you. I grew up with a father who prioritized money over everything else. Your dad was not that guy. He might have stood out there on the lake, spinning tales with you about fishing from the balcony of that cabin, but you missed the point of the story. He didn't need the cabin, because he already had what he wanted—he was already out there fishing with you."

Chloe shook her head, willing him to understand that she was on his side. She loved him and she wanted what was best for him. "I know everything you do is to make him proud—the truck you drive, the promotion you're after, the cabin you want to buy. You work long hours at a job that I'm not even sure you like. Do you honestly believe that's how the man in those photos would define success? Eighty-hour work weeks? A cookie-cutter show home but no one to share it with? No family of your own?"

A muscle ticked in Ben's jaw, and he got eerily calm. "Don't you dare stand there and act as if you know what my father would have wanted because you've looked at a couple of pictures." His words were a whip crack. Then he turned and stalked toward the bedroom, slamming the door in his wake.

Chloe stood there for a long moment, saddened that the Ben she'd met in Buffalo, the one she'd glimpsed the other night at Oz's house, the one she was sure his father would have been proud of, was slowly disappearing.

She was tempted to leave. Every muscle in her body was straining toward the door, but the ring on her finger was a stronger pull. She'd promised when she'd taken it from Ben that there would be no running this time. And she was going to be true to her word, because she was done with letting herself down.

She walked over to where her purse sat on the coffee table and pulled out her phone. She punched in the familiar number and brought it to her ear.

"Hey, Josh, it's me. Is Chad working tonight?...Great. Do you think you could call him and put in an order for six people?...Um, let's go with beef and chicken...Yes... Yep. And if he could whip up some of that incredible mushroom risotto of his...You know it. He can toss in two bottles of wine with that order as well, right?...And they deliver?...Oh, you will? Josh, you're the best! If you weren't gay I'd kiss you like I meant it. I'll text you the address. Seven o'clock would be perfect."

She rooted around in her bag until she located the book of matches that she carried for just such emergencies. With a steady hand, she lit the four vanilla-scented pillar candles she'd brought from her place the other day, and placed them strategically around the living room to help dissipate the smoky smell.

Then she grabbed her heels and dress from the front closet and headed toward the bathroom to change. She hooked her pearls around her neck as a final touch.

Then she returned to the living room to join Ben in stony silence as they waited for their guests to arrive.

## 15

BEN SWEPT THE door open to greet their visitors and Chloe plastered on her most gracious smile, ignoring the roiling in the pit of her stomach.

"Mr. McLeod, welcome." Ben shook the hand of a small man who Chloe would have mistaken for a funeral home director, if she'd guessed his profession on a plane. "Let me take your coat. This is my wife, Chloe."

His hand felt cold and dead in hers.

Ben had moved on to McLeod's wife. "Martine, you look lovely." He exchanged air kisses with a bony woman who proceeded to give Chloe a stern once-over and a weak handshake. Chloe could tell immediately that the McLeods were already not taken with her.

"Mr. Carson. Thank you for coming." The other boss. Used-car salesman-esque, with a big grin and a bigger gut. He used Chloe's hand like a pump handle and then ignored her completely.

Ben finished hanging their coats. "Sir, where's your lovely wife— Mel! What are you doing here?"

The sudden panic in Ben's voice drew Chloe's attention just as a beautiful blonde, looking impeccable in a trench coat, pumps and a wrap-dress, stepped into the condo. "Hello, Ben. It's been a while."

"I thought Elaine was coming?" Ben sounded a little gob-smacked, and was about two shades paler than he had been a moment ago.

"Mother was feeling a little under the weather today, so I offered to take her place."

"Just you? Where's your husband?" he asked, and Chloe was intrigued by the way Ben's voice hardened a little.

"Richard had a prior obligation." She smiled then, but it was cold. The other woman shrugged out of her jacket and handed it to Ben, but her eyes were on Chloe. "And speaking of significant others, aren't you going to introduce me to your wife?"

"Yes, of course." Ben slid the closet shut before stepping toward her. "Melanie, I'd like you to meet Chloe Masterson."

Chloe's heart stuttered.

*Melanie.*

Of course. Ben's fiancée. Well, ex-fiancée, but at least she'd been a real one at some point. Chloe unconsciously twisted the ring on her finger. Until she noticed Melanie's icy blue gaze on it.

"Melanie, nice to meet you," she said, remembering her manners.

"And you." The handshake was tense and appraising. Their pretty guest took a step toward the living room. "The place looks great. So different from your last condo."

Melanie's eyes cut to hers. Her ploy was obvious, but it still rankled.

"How about a tour?"

Melanie's question sounded sickly sweet to Chloe's ears, and she realized in that moment that if she didn't take control of this godforsaken party right then, it was going to spiral to its doom.

"What a lovely idea. Ben, why don't you show everyone around? I'm sure they'd love to see the place while we wait for dinner. But first, can I offer anyone an aperitif? I've got a lovely white chilling."

She'd caught the McLeods by surprise. She could see them reassessing her. Carson perked up at the mention of booze. "I'll take one!"

And Melanie, well, she was not impressed that Chloe had invited others to her private tour. Chloe smiled as she went back to the kitchen to pour. Maybe this wasn't going to be such a train wreck after all.

Chloe returned with a tray of wine, offering Martine and Melanie first selection, followed by McLeod and Carson.

"So I gotta ask, Chloe. What's with the hair? Couldn't afford the whole bottle of dye?" The big man's guffaws filled the condo. "Joking! I'm joking!"

Chloe bit back a hundred insults, laughing good-naturedly at the petty swipe. "Why, Mr. Carson. I would think a titan of the advertising world such as yourself would understand the value of standing out in a crowd," she chided.

The room went dead silent for a moment. Then Carson began to grin. "*Touché.* Spitfire you got here, Masterson. I like her moxie."

He took a big gulp of the expensive wine and Chloe let the last vestiges of nervousness slip away. She offered the last glass of wine on the tray to Ben, and when he accepted it, he was looking at her in a way he never had before.

"THE APARTMENT LOOKS LOVELY, Ben. Who's your decorator?"

They'd finished the brief tour, and dinner had arrived. The guy from the makeup store—Josh—was in the kitchen right now, transferring all the takeout from foam containers into real dishes. Ben had no idea when Chloe had arranged all that, and he couldn't ask her because right now she and Martine, an avid symphony fan, were discussing the classical music Chloe had turned on while he'd been showing everyone around the condo.

He wasn't quite sure how his "wife" had managed it, but things were going pretty well. Which was good, but it paled in comparison to how relieved he was that she hadn't up and walked out on him earlier.

"Ben?"

He started at the sound of Mel's voice. He'd forgotten she was there for a moment. "Is your mother really sick?"

Mel set the picture of him and his dad back on the bookshelf. "If I didn't know better, I might think you weren't happy to see me."

The evasion was classic Melanie, and he had his answer: Elaine was in perfect health.

She moved toward him, and he automatically stepped back.

"Has it come to that?" she asked quietly.

Ben wet his lips as she raised her hand to smooth the lapel of his Armani blazer. His gaze slipped to the gleaming diamonds that decorated her left ring finger, so different than the ring he'd offered her.

He'd met her during his second week with Carson and McLeod. She'd made fun of his suit—it had cost him five hundred dollars, which was the most he'd ever spent on an item of clothing in his life. The gibes had been the first salvos in a courtship that, in retrospect, had consisted of Ben doing his very best to impress her and Melanie remaining dutifully unimpressed to ensure he would continue to try.

Today, for the first time since he'd met her, he didn't care what she thought. The realization was freeing.

"You slowpokes comin' for dinner? We're starving over here!"

The smile Mel shot him was almost regretful, but he wasn't sure why. "Coming, Daddy."

They settled into the business *and* the dinner immediately, with Carson and McLeod tag-teaming him with questions that were designed to figure out where he stood on issues the firm was facing. Every once in a while he was able to take a bite of incredible food, from beef bourguignon to mushroom risotto.

They didn't ask him anything he wasn't expecting, which meant that in between the "Yes, Mr. Carson, I definitely think that the A/B testing warrants a re-evaluation of Sports Nation's decision to rebrand," and the "No, Mr. McLeod, the mock-ups for the Delaney account won't be ready in time for the general meeting," Ben had enough focus left over to monitor how things were going at the other end of the table.

Which was not well.

"THE FOOD IS EXQUISITE, my dear," Mrs. McLeod complimented, and Chloe was thankful that she was friends with someone as talented as Chad in the kitchen. Otherwise they'd be having pepperoni pizza or Chinese takeout.

"I'd love to take credit for it, but who has time to cook?"

It was a standard joke amongst *ladies who lunched*, and Martine smiled knowingly—the acceptable response—but it seemed Melanie wasn't here to play nice.

"What is it that you do again?"

Chloe raised her eyebrows at the violation of manners. "I'm sorry?"

"Well, you implied you don't have time to cook. I was just wondering what it was that took up so much of your day," Melanie asked.

"Actually, I—"

"Chloe is an incredible makeup artist," Ben interrupted, and Chloe clenched her hands into fists in an attempt to keep calm. A lady did not show emotion in public. A fact for which Ben should be ever-freaking-grateful for right about now.

"She's got a growing following on YouTube and she's poised to create a big splash in the industry."

"Makeup. How...*fanciful*."

As far as insults went, Melanie's polite dismissal was pretty much the worst Chloe could think of.

"I mean, I'm envious!" the other woman added. "I would love to play dress-up all the time. Maybe in my next life. For now, I guess being a lawyer will have to do."

The rest of the dinner guests had the grace to look uncomfortable at the breach of etiquette.

"I'm also on the board of the Girls Have Power Foundation."

"Oh? How interesting. What's that all about?" It galled Chloe to ask, to allow Melanie to preen in the spotlight. But tonight was about Ben, and she wasn't going to screw it up for him, even if he'd been a self-righteous prick earlier.

"Our goal is to improve the futures of girls by elevating their self-esteem, helping them get through school and encouraging them to take on the world as successful women. We do all sorts of networking events and workshops, and we also bring in speakers on a variety of issues that affect the girls."

"Chloe did an amazing set of makeup videos about

self-esteem, calling out cosmetic companies for all the false advertising they do in their ads and commercials."

Chloe glared at Ben.

"How lovely that your little makeup videos are so ambitious. But I hardly think teaching our young ladies how to apply bronzer is going to help them in the long run."

*Me. Ow.* Chloe's resolve to play nice snapped. *Oh, it's on now.*

"With all due respect, Melanie, I disagree wholeheartedly. Makeup can be an incredibly powerful tool to help women raise their self-esteem."

Melanie's "Oh?" was derisive.

"I'm not claiming it's magical. I agree that it's a huge problem when companies trade on unrealistic beauty ideals to sell their products. But that's why it's so important to educate girls about the truth of advertising. It's empowering, for example, to know that when your eyes don't look like the models' after you apply their 'miracle' product, that's got nothing to do with you. You're fine just the way you are."

"Surely you're not suggesting that wearing makeup is equivalent to graduating high school or getting a good job."

"Of course not! But if you feel beautiful, it can be just the boost you need to walk into a job interview with confidence and nail it. And I know you're not implying that physical appearance doesn't matter because I can see that *you* are wearing makeup today. Why is that?"

Melanie's eyes narrowed, and Chloe took a sip of wine to keep from sticking her tongue out at the woman.

"I think we're veering away from the point," Ben offered, obviously trying to get this dinner party back on the rails. He turned to Carson and McLeod. "This, right here, is the kind of cross-marketing and co-branding opportunity I'd recommend we take better advantage of if I'm chosen for the new position. Imagine the power of connecting our clients, instead of keeping everyone separate."

The men launched back into shop talk. Melanie remained focused on her risotto, and Martine filled the conversational chasm with interesting facts about the Vivaldi piece that was playing in the background.

The rest of the evening passed without incident, but she was relieved when their sham finally came to an end.

"Chloe, it was a pleasure meeting you. Such a lovely dinner. You've done your husband proud."

Mr. McLeod's old-fashioned compliment landed with a thud in Chloe's gut. "Thank you, sir. And thank you so much for coming. Let me get your coats," she offered.

"Ben," Carson boomed. "Very impressive dinner to go with your very impressive work this year. You didn't hear it from me, but let me just say that you're going to be a very happy man when you arrive at the office on Monday morning." Carson slapped Ben on the back as he passed him.

As the rest of their guests filed out, Chloe thought briefly of her mother, wondering how she'd handled so much bullshit on a regular basis during her twenty-eight years of marriage.

Because she'd loved Daryl Masterson, she realized. But if tonight had taught Chloe anything, it was that she needed more than that. Pretending to be this person may have landed her the hot businessman and the parental acceptance, but if they weren't true to themselves and each other, what did it matter if she loved him?

BEN CLOSED THE door behind his guests and leaned back against it. A slow smile dawned on his face. They'd done it. Despite the fighting and the chicken and Melanie, somehow Chloe had managed to throw the best damn dinner party he'd ever been to, and now all his hard work was paying off.

"Did you hear that? I got the job!"

"Congratulations." The word came out cool.

He didn't blame Chloe for being mad at him. He'd said some awful things, and then she'd had to deal with Melanie. But he would never have been able to pull this night off alone. He owed a lot to the woman standing across from him.

"You were incredible tonight, Chloe. Seriously. You totally saved my ass, and I really appreciate it. This promotion has been my whole world, and it never would have happened without you."

"Ben, I have to go."

"What? But you and I have some celebrating to do!"

"I'm happy for you. If this is the life you want, then congratulations. Enjoy it. But it's not the one I want. In fact, it's exactly what I ran away from."

"What are you saying?"

"You're not the same guy I met on the plane. Or the guy I hung out with at Amy's birthday party."

He frowned. "Sure I am."

She shook her head. "That guy would never have jumped into the middle of a conversation and told a bunch of complete strangers about my hopes and dreams just to save his own pride."

It felt like she'd slapped him. "Chloe, I didn't—"

"We don't want the same things, Ben. If this was what I wanted, you and I would never have met. I would be Mrs. Patrick McQuaid and I'd be celebrating my fourth wedding anniversary. And what I was trying to say earlier is that it's not really what you want, either. But you can't see that beyond your grief and your ego. So I'm going to go pack my stuff now. "

Ben was numb. He couldn't believe she was going to walk out on him like this. Didn't she understand that he'd just landed his big break? How good it would be for him? How good it could be for them?

She reappeared a few minutes later, pulling her suitcase behind her, her purse slung over her shoulder. She stopped beside him.

"Congratulations on the promotion. I'm really happy that things worked out for you."

"Don't go." It was all he could say. It made her pause, but just for a second.

"I have to." Tears welled in her eyes and it took everything he had not to grab her and hold onto her with everything he had. But she'd made her choice.

She notched her chin up and strode away from him, right out the front door.

And, for the second time, he let her go.

# *16*

His chair felt weird.

Ben bounced up and down on it a few times, spun it side to side.

It was exactly like the chair in his old office, but something was off. He'd been fiddling with it all week to no avail.

In an attempt to ignore the vast piles of paperwork crowding his desk—account directors spent far more time with file folders than human beings—Ben glanced around his new corner office. But instead of admiring his beautiful view of downtown Seattle, his gaze focused on the picture he'd hung on the dull gray wall across from his desk. The frame was crooked again.

Ben got up and walked over, nudging the bottom right corner higher so that he and his dad and the cabin were square.

"So what do you think, Pop? Pretty fancy digs, huh?"

The picture tilted listlessly to the right in response. Ben nodded. "I hear ya."

He pulled the frame off the wall just as a knock sounded on the door. He could tell by the timid rap that it was his new assistant. Lana had always burst right in.

"Come on in, Nancy."

"Mr. Masterson—"

"Just Ben," he reminded her, walking back to his desk. The brunette smiled shyly before proceeding to call him nothing at all. "Mr. Carson and Mr. McLeod would like to see you in Mr. Carson's office as soon as possible. Also, a Mr. Laroche from Allies Real Estate called about some lakefront property. He's asked you to call him back at this number when you're free."

Ben accepted the yellow message slip. "Thanks."

She dipped her head and disappeared out the door.

Ben glanced at the paper and dropped it onto his desk.

With the framed photo still clutched in his right hand, he headed to his boss's office.

Carson's assistant, Doris, was on the phone, but she waved him in as soon as he'd exited the elevator. He smiled his thanks and stepped through the glass door.

"There's our new account director!" Rob Carson was as genial as ever. "Have a seat."

Ben sat in the leather visitor's chair, placing the frame on his lap. "Mr. Carson. Mr. McLeod," he greeted. "Before we begin, I just want to take this chance to thank you both for this amazing promotion and to let you know that I'm resigning, effective immediately."

"I'm sorry, what did you just say?"

Ben exhaled and straightened his tie. "I said I quit."

Carson turned a shade of tomato that probably didn't bode well for his blood pressure, and Hugh McLeod was so still that Ben couldn't be certain he hadn't calcified.

"I really appreciate the opportunities you have given me, and I've learned a lot here, but creating ad campaigns isn't what I want to do with my life. Chloe's been trying to tell me that all along, but I was too blinded by pride to see that she was right. I don't belong here."

"Your wife told you to quit?" Carson demanded.

"Oh, she's not my wife," Ben corrected him. "We met on my business trip to Buffalo. But when Edward Burke came to my hotel room that morning, well, I did what I had to do to get his business."

"So you've been lying to us ever since you landed the Hotel Burke account?"

Ben nodded. "Pretty much."

"That dedication is exactly what we like about you, Ben. You do whatever it takes to close a deal," McLeod said matter-of-factly. "Which is why we offered you this job."

"And ironically, that's why I'm turning it down. Because I don't want to be a guy who lies, especially to myself. I want to help people grow their ideas into something special. I want to run a business built on integrity, one that I can be proud of. And that's why I can't accept this promotion."

Ben reached into the breast pocket of his gray suit—the one he'd worn the day he'd met Chloe—and pulled out an envelope. He slid it onto Rob Carson's desk as he stood.

"Now if you gentlemen will excuse me, I need to get to the mall."

"Not so fast," Carson said, picking up his phone. "Yes, security? We're going to need a walk-out on the tenth floor."

With a maniacal sigh, Ben sat back down.

"RECEIPT IN THE bag okay?" At the woman's nod, Chloe handed over the purchase. "Here you go. Enjoy your new eye shadow palette and thank you for shopping at Titanium Beauty."

Chloe's salesgirl smile faded the moment the woman turned away from the counter. Monday was dragging.

"Josh, I'm going on my break," she called, and he nodded. Chloe grabbed her purse from the back room and headed out into the mall, toward the food court.

There was a gaggle of teenage girls chatting by one of the fountains, and Chloe slurped at the cardboard keg of cola she'd just purchased, trying her best not to give in to self-pity. But being on lunch break at her mall job, her name tag pinned above her left boob, didn't make her feel like she'd reached the pinnacle of achievement, that was for sure.

Her makeup application with Joanna, though—now that had felt like a real accomplishment. Joanna had been really happy with the results, and just the memory of the consultation made her sit a bit taller. But one paying gig wasn't going to keep a roof over her head, so until she could grow her business, Chloe had decided Titanium Beauty was preferable to unemployment. And the makeup discount was nice.

Chloe sighed. A big unapologetic one. Because Ben would have hated it. And because he was right. She had been taking the easy way out. Chloe grabbed her phone out of her purse and dialed.

"Hello?"

"Hi, Mom."

"What's wrong? Why are you calling me? You never call me."

Chloe resisted the urge to say something snarky. This was about the truth. "Nothing's wrong, Mom. I just felt like calling." As much as she'd hated that business dinner and the persona she'd so easily slipped into, the experience had also given her some insight into her mother. So she supposed some good had come out of the bad.

"Chloe Marie, I'm your mother. I know it pains you to admit that, but I am. And I can tell when you're not okay."

"It's just…" Chloe gazed down at her left hand. The stupid ring had been haunting her all week. She hated wearing it, but she couldn't take it off. "It's Ben."

"Did you two have a fight? I know that can be upsetting, but all couples have their spats."

*Now or never.* "We're not engaged."

"You broke up?"

"No, Mom. We were never dating. It was a lie. I lied to you. I was helping him out because his bosses heard he was married, and then Caroline saw the ring and, well, you two were so happy with me, and I just…let you go on believing it."

"You're not engaged? But, Chloe, he was so good for you!"

Chloe's laugh sounded bitter, even to her. "Yes, he was good for *me*. Gainfully employed and well-mannered with a closet full of designer suits. In short, the perfect son-in-law. Everything *I'm* looking for in a man."

A tense silence descended, so thick it seemed to Chloe that even the ambient food court noise had been muted. Then, in a soft voice she barely recognized as her mother's, "You always think the worst of me, don't you?"

The question took Chloe aback.

"I find Benjamin," there was a deep breath on the other end of the line, "Ben," she said pointedly, "to be personable and quite in love with my daughter. So yes. He has my approval. Not that you care a whit about that. But when I said he was good for you, I meant that he's good for *you*. You're happy when you're with him. Vibrant. Not my complicated little girl anymore. A woman."

Chloe ran her index finger along her cup, tracing a line in the condensation.

"Despite what you believe, Chloe, despite the clashes in our ideologies and the differences in our priorities, you're my daughter and I just want the best for you. And I know that means I have to stay out of your life and let you make your own choices. Which is very difficult for me. But I'm trying. Because I want you to be happy."

Chloe went still for a moment and she had to try twice to get any words to come out. "Thank you, Mom. That means a lot."

"Now, all that being said, do not ruin this relationship. Ben is the most appropriate man who's been interested in you since I set you up with Bryce Willington Jr. just before you moved to Seattle. Now *he* was quite the catch. Muriel's daughter scooped him right up after you left. I told you someone would! And I—"

"Gotta get back to work, Mom. Thanks for the chat." Chloe ended the call, a million thoughts whirling through her head.

She looked down at her left hand. At the ring she couldn't bring herself to take off. And why? Because her fake engagement to Ben was the best relationship she'd ever been in. If Ben had taught her anything, it was that sometimes you just had to seize the opportunity that was in front of you.

Because, as it turned out, her mother was right. Ben *was* good for her.

She'd known it from the start. She'd just been too scared to believe it.

But she wasn't scared anymore.

UNLIKE THE LAST time Ben had been here, Titanium Beauty was empty today. He was relieved to recognize the employee standing at the cash register, flipping though a magazine.

"Hey, you're Chloe's friend. Josh, right? Thanks for helping us out on Saturday night."

The other man stared at him for a long, silent moment, then said, "Ohmygawd."

"I, uh… I'm looking for Chloe. Have you seen her?"

"Ohmygawd! You are not going to believe this, but you just missed her. Like *just* missed her. She came running back from her break to grab her coat because she was going to find you!" Josh sighed. "I'm living in a rom-com."

"Do you know where she went?"

"No idea, big guy. She just said, 'I'm going to find Ben,' and took off."

Well, she was either headed to his place or to his work. And since he was not technically allowed on the premises of Carson and McLeod, he supposed that left him only one destination.


"I'M LOOKING FOR Ben Masterson."

The receptionist at the posh offices of Carson and McLeod shot her such a bored glare that Chloe half expected her to whip out a nail file, just to perfect the tableau. "May I ask what this is about?"

"I just need to see my… I need to talk to Ben. Is he here?"

The woman sighed and just for a moment there was a glimpse of sadness in her pretty face. "I'm afraid not. Mr. Masterson no longer works at Carson and McLeod."

"I'm sorry?"

"Mr. Masterson is no longer employed at the firm. I'm afraid I can't give you any further information."

"But I have to find him. Did he go home? Is he okay?"

Chloe's genuine panic seemed to strike a chord with the brunette. Her eyes dropped briefly to Chloe's chest, and Chloe realized she'd forgotten to remove her name tag. "You're her. The girl Ben was looking for last week!"

And just like that, she and the secretary were old friends. The woman leaned forward in her chair and lowered her voice conspiratorially. "Look, you didn't hear this from me, but from what I've gathered, he got called into Carson's office this morning to sign all the papers for his promotion to account director, but instead he quit. The big boss men were not amused, and some yelling ensued, but Ben wouldn't back down. Then he got frog-marched off the property.

"It's against company policy for terminated employees to talk to anyone on their way out of the building, so when you find him, be sure to tell him Lana misses him, okay?"

"Sure. And thank you."

"No problem. And killer makeup, by the way."

Chloe rushed back to the elevator and hit the down button a couple of times in quick succession.

Ben didn't work here anymore? She worried her bottom lip. Was this because of her? If his bosses had discovered they weren't really married, that the entire dinner had been a sham, they might have—

The metal doors slid open with a ding, interrupting her thoughts. And then she recognized the lone occupant of the elevator.

*Great.*

"Chloe?"

Melanie. Looking perfect and lawyerly in a skirt, heels and a fancy black coat with leather trim. Her hair was perfect, her makeup flawless—if a little tame—and she was carrying a freaking briefcase!

Chloe snatched her Titanium Beauty name tag off with undue haste. The magnet that had held it in place slipped down the front of her shirt and bounced on the carpet. She abandoned it in the name of retaining some modicum of cool. "Oh, hey."

"Hi! What a surprise. I was just dropping something off for my father."

Chloe shrugged ambivalently, but stepped inside, cursing her horrible timing as the elevator doors slid closed behind her. Her name plate bit into her palm, she was fisting it so tightly.

"I didn't expect you to come here, now that Ben, well… What *are* you doing here, anyway?" Melanie asked. Chloe could see the questions in her eyes.

"Ben left something behind," Chloe said, not willing to admit that she wasn't his wife and was unaware he didn't work here anymore. Not to this woman who'd been so condescending. "A pair of cuff links that he really likes. A lot. He thought he might have left them in his desk…when he was, uh, packing his stuff up…and I was in the neighborhood, so I figured I'd check for him. You know. Wife stuff."

"Of course. Wife stuff." Melanie dropped her eyes to her briefcase. And then, in a rush she said, "Chloe, I just wanted to apologize for my behavior the other night. I was way out of line."

Chloe blinked. She certainly hadn't been expecting that. "No big deal."

"It was. I'm a lawyer who built a name for herself defending feminism, and the next thing I know, I'm acting like a total bitch to my ex-boyfriend's new wife."

Chloe couldn't have been more shocked if Melanie had punched her in the face. In fact, an elevator brawl seemed a more plausible scenario.

"I was jealous. So I elbowed my way into your home, and when I saw you wearing the ring, the ring he bought for me... Well, we're very different people, aren't we?" she asked.

Chloe looked down at her companion's perfectly manicured fingers, polished in a pale shade of pink. A ginormous engagement ring–wedding band combo glittered on her ring finger. From the man she'd chosen over Ben. Stupid mistake. Because Ben was amazing, and Melanie hadn't noticed. But Chloe had. And she was going to do something about it. "Yeah. We really are."

"But I can tell you two belong together. You bring out this side of him, this fearless side." Melanie laughed, but it was forced. "I mean, do you know how long I tried to get him to decorate his last condo?"

The elevator opened and they stepped into the bustling lobby.

"I acted like a petulant child whose toy had been stolen, and I am not only embarrassed, I'm deeply sorry. I hope you can forgive me."

"Sure, yes. Thank you." Chloe nodded, unwillingly impressed with the woman in front of her. "And I'm sorry too. For being a jerk. And for thinking you were a stuck-up bitch."

Melanie's chuckle was genuine this time. "I appreciate that. And Chloe? Take care of him. Ben's one of the good guys." With that, she turned and strode out of the building and disappeared into the chilly Seattle morning.

It was, Chloe figured, the most grown-up conversation she'd ever taken part in. And it felt pretty damn good. Like she could handle anything.

Including getting her fiancé back.

# 17

CHLOE CRAWLED OUT of the cab with several bags of Chinese takeout. She hoped the food might keep Ben from slamming the door in her face. With a deep breath to calm the flipping of her stomach, she walked into the foyer of the building.

She was debating the merits of calling him on the phone versus ringing the buzzer when she remembered she still had his keys.

*Here goes nothing.* With a deep breath, she let herself into the building.

By the time she got to his door, her heart was a jackhammer in her chest. And not because of her power walk from the elevator, either. She knocked on the door before her nerves could talk her out of it.

The door flew open alarmingly fast. Almost as though he'd been waiting for her. He looked unbearably handsome in the gray suit and blue tie he'd been wearing the first day they'd met. "Hi."

"Hi."

She held up the peace offering. "I brought you some lunch."

Ben's face fell, and it made her heart squeeze. "Oh."

He invited her in with a sweep of his hand. She stepped into the familiar apartment—had she really only stayed here for a week? He took the bags of takeout from her and headed into the living room.

So much awkwardness in so little space. This was harder than she'd thought it would be.

"I went by your office to see you," she said, desperate to break the uncomfortable silence that was stifling them. "Well, your former office, I guess."

Ben nodded as he unpacked the cartons of food, spreading them out on the coffee table. "Yeah, I quit. I didn't want to end up being the kind of person who smothers dreams. I'd rather create them."

He straightened, surveying the boxes that represented about two-thirds of the Mr. Chow menu.

"I'm starting my own company. Masterson Creative Group. I want to help people take their small businesses to the next level, but I'm going to do some consulting for larger firms until I'm solvent," he told her. "Hotel Burke is looking over my proposal right now. We'll see how it plays out."

"What about the cabin?"

"Someone pointed out to me that the real fun is on the lake, not in some swanky cabin."

"Your father would be very proud of you, Ben."

He shrugged, like it wasn't a big deal, but she could see his pride in the set of his shoulders and the tilt of his chin. "I think you're right."

"I'm really proud of you, too."

The sudden quiet made it hard to breathe.

"Chloe?"

His voice was soft and low, and for the first time Chloe could remember, he sounded uncertain.

"Don't take this the wrong way, but what are you doing here?"

"I just…there's something I need to know."

He opened his arms in a *just ask* gesture.

"Why didn't you tell her?" She held up her hand. "Why didn't you tell Melanie this was your grandma's ring?"

He shook his head, a slight frown marring his forehead. "I'm not sure. I've wondered about that a lot. Especially over the past week."

"You told me."

Ben nodded. "I wanted you to know."

Chloe tried to absorb the words, to force them to make sense. "We'd only just met when you put this on my finger."

He raked a hand through his hair. "I don't have any explanations for you and me. It shouldn't work. You said it yourself. You've spent your whole life running away from the stuff I've been working toward. But we do work. Somehow all that other stuff doesn't seem to matter."

Chloe's skin pricked to life even as she tried to hold her hope in check.

"I'm so sorry I hurt you, Chloe. You're right. I was trying to impress them because I thought that was the life I wanted. But it's not. Especially not if it's going to make me act like a raging douchebag. But I meant every word I said. I didn't spin anything. I just told them the truth. You *are* an incredible makeup artist. It's what you should be doing with your life. And don't let the fact that I got carried away trying to make some ignorant old fools see how amazing you are cloud the issue."

Chloe sat heavily on the couch and bit her lip. "Do not make me cry, Masterson."

"I guess what I'm trying to say is that I love the mess

you've made of my bathroom counter. And I love how every time you mention your hair, you pull a piece forward and stare at it, as if you're judging it for yourself. I love that you chew your right thumbnail when you're nervous. And I love that you've brought color to my living room. And to my life."

Ben got down on one knee and grabbed her left hand in his, and Chloe laughed through her impending tears.

"I realize we haven't known each other for very long, but I like you a lot, Chloe Masterson. In fact, I'm pretty sure I'm completely and totally in love with you. So will you do me the honor of unmarrying me?"

He slipped his grandma's ring off her finger, and with it went the pressure and the lies. Chloe's hand suddenly felt as light as her mood. Although her eyes still stung a little.

Romance was making her soft. And she'd never been happier.

"I love you, too, Masterson. And I'd be honored to unmarry you."

His lopsided grin stole her breath. "Then it's settled. We'll start over."

She crinkled up her nose. "Like in all the girly movies?"

He grinned at the reference. "Just like that, Latoya."

"C'mere, Julio." She fisted her hand in the crew neck of his T-shirt, tugging him closer.

"Careful. This T-shirt cost an obscene amount of money."

"I'll bet it did," she said, breaching the space between them to touch her lips to his. To kiss Ben like it was the first night, when nothing was hanging over their heads except possibilities.

And great sex.

He stood up, pulling her to her feet, and then right off them and into his arms. She wrapped her legs around his waist as he started walking them toward the bedroom.

"So, listen, I don't usually mix business with pleasure, but as the owner of a struggling start-up, I could really use a client who's poised on the brink of success."

He set her down in front of the bedroom.

"Makeup by Chloe is a business built on integrity. We frown on nepotism. You're going to have to really wow me if you want the job."

"Okay, picture this—a campaign with the tagline 'Kiss and Makeup.'"

"You make a strong case, Masterson." Chloe grabbed Ben's hand and tugged him into the bedroom. "I think we should definitely get started on that right away."

\* \* \* \* \*

## #867 THE MIGHTY QUINNS: MAC
*The Mighty Quinns*
### by Kate Hoffmann

Emma Bryant wants a passionate, no-strings affair, and she's found the perfect man to seduce—bad-boy pilot Luke MacKenzie. At least, he would be perfect...if he didn't suddenly want more from Emma than a casual fling.

## #868 UNDER PRESSURE
*SEALs of Fortune*
### by Kira Sinclair

Former Navy SEAL Asher Reynolds isn't afraid of anything—except being on camera. Too bad his best friend's little sister, Kennedy Duchane, is determined to have him star in a documentary...and in her sexiest fantasies!

## #869 A WRONG BED CHRISTMAS
*The Wrong Bed*
### by Kimberly Van Meter and Liz Talley

Two firefighters, two mix-ups, two happily-ever-afters? Celebrate the holidays with two scorching-hot Wrong Bed stories in one!

## #870 A DANGEROUSLY SEXY CHRISTMAS
### by Stefanie London

Max Ridgeway has sworn to protect Rose Lawson, even if she doesn't want him to. But the beautiful Rose is temptation personified, and Max walks a razor-thin line between keeping her safe and giving in to his desire...

---

HBCNM1015

# REQUEST YOUR FREE BOOKS!
## 2 FREE NOVELS PLUS 2 FREE GIFTS!

**HARLEQUIN®**

*Blaze®*

### red-hot reads!

**YES!** Please send me 2 FREE Harlequin® Blaze® novels and my 2 FREE gifts (gifts are worth about $10). After receiving them, if I don't wish to receive any more books, I can return the shipping statement marked "cancel." If I don't cancel, I will receive 4 brand-new novels every month and be billed just $4.74 per book in the U.S. or $5.21 per book in Canada. That's a savings of at least 14% off the cover price. It's quite a bargain. Shipping and handling is just 50¢ per book in the U.S. and 75¢ per book in Canada.* I understand that accepting the 2 free books and gifts places me under no obligation to buy anything. I can always return a shipment and cancel at any time. Even if I never buy another book, the two free books and gifts are mine to keep forever.

150/350 HDN GH2D

| | | |
|---|---|---|
| Name | (PLEASE PRINT) | |
| Address | | Apt. # |
| City | State/Prov. | Zip/Postal Code |

Signature (if under 18, a parent or guardian must sign)

### Mail to the **Reader Service**:
**IN U.S.A.:** P.O. Box 1867, Buffalo, NY 14240-1867
**IN CANADA:** P.O. Box 609, Fort Erie, Ontario L2A 5X3

**Want to try two free books from another line?**
**Call 1-800-873-8635 or visit www.ReaderService.com.**

* Terms and prices subject to change without notice. Prices do not include applicable taxes. Sales tax applicable in N.Y. Canadian residents will be charged applicable taxes. Offer not valid in Quebec. This offer is limited to one order per household. Not valid for current subscribers to Harlequin Blaze books. All orders subject to credit approval. Credit or debit balances in a customer's account(s) may be offset by any other outstanding balance owed by or to the customer. Please allow 4 to 6 weeks for delivery. Offer available while quantities last.

**Your Privacy**—The Reader Service is committed to protecting your privacy. Our Privacy Policy is available online at www.ReaderService.com or upon request from the Reader Service.

We make a portion of our mailing list available to reputable third parties that offer products we believe may interest you. If you prefer that we not exchange your name with third parties, or if you wish to clarify or modify your communication preferences, please visit us at www.ReaderService.com/consumerschoice or write to us at Reader Service Preference Service, P.O. Box 9062, Buffalo, NY 14240-9062. Include your complete name and address.

HB15

*Kennedy Duchane and Asher Reynolds have been fighting their attraction for years. But when she has to help him overcome stage fright, a little sexy distraction may be just the ticket!*

*Read on for a sneak preview of*
*UNDER PRESSURE,*
*the final book in* **Kira Sinclair**'s *sizzling trilogy*
*SEALS OF FORTUNE.*

The sweet scent of vanilla tickled Asher Reynolds's senses.

Cracking one eye open, he stared up at Kennedy Duchane looming above him. Her thighs were spread on either side of his hips.

"I could get used to waking up to this, Cupcake," he rumbled, threading his fingers through her hair and pulling her closer.

Something soft and wet swept across his cheek.

"What the hell?"

She grinned wickedly, and for the first time he realized she held something in her hand. A pale cupcake with a thick swirl of bright pink frosting.

Eyeing it, he asked, "What is that?"

Her grin widened. "Payback."

Before he could even twitch, the thing was top-down in his face. Kennedy smeared the sticky mess from his forehead, down his nose and across his chin.

There was no question, he was under siege.

Asher grabbed her by the waist and flipped her onto her back. He wasn't about to make this easy.

With one hand, he captured her wrist, holding her arm above her head and immobilizing her weapon of choice.

She hadn't just brought one, but a full dozen of the sticky pink things.

Stretching out, he grabbed some ammunition of his own and struck. She yelped in surprise and tried to wiggle away. But he had her well and truly pinned.

"Nowhere to go, Sugar," he drawled.

Kennedy glared up. "Calling me Sugar is no better than calling me Cupcake, you Southern-fried Neanderthal."

Dipping his finger in the pink confection, Asher spread a smear across her collarbone.

"I only use nicknames with people I actually like," he murmured.

She squirmed. "Why Cupcake? It sounds so…empty-headed and pointless."

"Hardly." Pushing up onto his elbows, Asher gazed at her, his heart thumping erratically.

"*Cupcake* is the perfect description for you, Kennedy. The kind of treat you know you shouldn't want, but you can't seem to stop craving… Besides, I always knew you'd taste so damn sweet." He brushed his lips over her frosting-covered skin.

*Don't miss*
*UNDER PRESSURE by Kira Sinclair*
*available November 2015 wherever*
*Harlequin® Blaze® books and ebooks are sold.*

www.Harlequin.com

HBEXP1015

# Love the Harlequin book you just read?

Your opinion matters.

Review this book on your favorite book site, review site, blog or your own social media properties and share your opinion with other readers!

# Turn your love of reading into rewards you'll love with
# Harlequin My Rewards